NANCY WARREN

GARTERS AND GARGOYLES

VAMPIRE KNITTING CLUB
BOOK TEN

ISBN: ebook 978-1-928145-75-2

ISBN: print 978-1-928145-74-5

Cover Design by Lou Harper of Cover Affairs

Ambleside Publishing

INTRODUCTION

A Secret Society leads to Murder

The Gargoyle Club is a secret society in Oxford's Cardinal College, where privileged young men from important families get drunk and rowdy and cause trouble. Rafe, as a member of the club, is not impressed with these newest Gargoyles.

Meanwhile, a social climbing high school friend of Lucy's is in town. Is she really after an art history degree or is her purpose more devious?

When someone dies during a club dinner it looks like more than boys behaving badly. It's up to Lucy and her undead knitters to solve the crime.

~

Get the origin story of Rafe, the gorgeous, sexy vampire in *The Vampire Knitting Club* series, for free when you join Nancy's no-spam newsletter at NancyWarrenAuthor.com.

Come join Nancy in her private Facebook group where we talk about books, knitting, pets and life.
www.facebook.com/groups/NancyWarrenKnitwits

GARTERS AND GARGOYLES

*R*afe tossed the newspaper aside in disgust. "In my day, secret societies were exactly that, secret. None of this showing up on the front page of the newspaper looking drunk and disorderly."

I was busy restocking the shelves of Cardinal Woolsey's Knitting and Yarn shop, but at the words "secret society," I had to look over his shoulder. Something about the notion intrigued me. Probably because I was pretty sure I'd never be invited to any secret club. Unless you counted my local coven, which I wasn't invited to join as much as forced into by my annoying witch relatives.

The front page of the *Oxford Daily* showed a fuzzy photograph of four young men looking definitely the worse for wear. One appeared to be peeing into the bushes outside a very nice house. Behind them was a broken window. The headline read: "Rowdy Youth Damage Oxford Property." I skimmed the article, but it was only a couple of paragraphs about how these young men had disrupted a quiet neighborhood, vandalized property and police believed a young woman had witnessed their behavior. They were looking for help in identifying the men and wanted the young woman to come forward to help with their inquiries.

"There's nothing there about any secret society," I said, disappointed. I wanted to read about bizarre midnight rituals and feasts that lasted days. This just looked like a stag party gone wrong.

Rafe shook his head at me. "There used to be dignity and honor associated with The Order of the Gargoyles. Now it's nothing but rich lads with weak heads and no morals."

I had to hold back my laugh. "Order of the Gargoyles?" Was he kidding me?

When he gave me that snooty look down the length of his nose, I had to ask. "Were you in this secret club, Rafe?"

"It's a very old order that's long existed at Cardinal College. Technically, I still am a member."

I glanced at the paper and back at him. His jaw was set, and he looked very peeved. "Do you know those kids?"

"Oh, yes. And I think it's time I paid them a visit."

He looked so forbidding, I put a hand on the sleeve of his navy cashmere sweater. "What are you going to do?"

"Nothing like what they deserve." With that, I had to be contented, as he left Cardinal Woolsey's with a determined stride. I ran to the window and watched him head in the direction of Cardinal College.

A FEW DAYS LATER, I was holding the door open for a woman who'd made the trip to Oxford specially to visit Cardinal

Woolsey's. An avid knitter, she'd stocked up, buying so much wool and patterns and magazines that her arms were too full to manage the door. I was delighted.

After we'd said our last goodbyes, I went back inside, reminding myself it was really time I put out another newsletter. I should also update our website. People all around the world shopped at my store, some bought online and some would drive miles to come here in person. The online store was a growing and valuable part of my business.

I usually did that kind of work at night, but I was making notes when the cheerful bells went, signaling I had a new customer. I turned with a smile of welcome on my face, which froze when I recognized the woman who entered. She was tall and slim, with long, dark hair, intense, dark eyes, and a face that at first glance appeared beautiful but was really perhaps more stunning. She did everything she could with that face, making up her dark eyes with darker shadow and keeping her lipstick fresh and her hair nearly always newly brushed. Her wardrobe was expensive and meant not to look that way. Her name was Pamela Black, and she was one of the last people I'd expected or wanted to see. Ever.

She smiled a bright, happy smile and came toward me with her arms out. "Lucy. I couldn't believe it when I heard you were here in Oxford. One of my best friends ever. I'm so excited to see you."

Before I could do anything more than gape helplessly at her, she was wrapping me in her arms. I smelled the familiar scent of her and felt myself gag.

I pulled away as soon as I could. "Pamela. What are you doing here?"

It would be foolish to say that I had left Boston and come

to England to escape anyone. Well, okay, there'd been the heartache over discovering that Todd, my boyfriend, wasn't exactly true blue. But now that some time had passed, I saw him for the jerk he was and knew I'd had a lucky escape.

Pamela was the kind of person that, once she'd drawn you into her web and pretty much sucked the life out of you, all you wanted to do was escape. Far away. Forever.

If I'd thought about it, I was relieved to live thousands of miles away from the woman who'd broken my heart far more thoroughly than Todd ever could.

Pamela seemed to have completely forgotten the past. How convenient. Or she chose to either ignore it or pretend it had never happened. Worse, she likely thought it meant nothing to me. As it most likely did to her.

We'd been sixteen years old. I'd never have called her my best friend, but we'd been close. I'd been giddy in love with a guy named Sam. He wasn't the best-looking guy; he wasn't the smartest or most athletic. He was quirky. Different. Funny. He drew cartoons—that's how uncool he was.

I don't know what it was that made Pamela decide she wanted Sam. In my narcissistic moments, I suspected she only wanted him because he was mine. Even now, with the hindsight of more than ten years' experience, I still wasn't certain if that was why she'd gone after my boyfriend.

A classic frenemy, she'd come to me, when she and Sam first started going out together. Sat me down. "Oh, Lucy, I need to know you're okay with this. You know Sam and I would never do anything to hurt you. You're my best friend. It's just that—" She'd giggled. "It's so overwhelming. I know you only want the best for both of us. We'll always be friends. Right?"

I was stunned, and brokenhearted, and there was a fierce pride inside me that refused to let her see how hurt I was. And perhaps she was right. What did I know about love? I didn't own Sam. If their hearts belonged to each other, maybe I needed to be the bigger person.

And I really tried to be that bigger person, as much as I could at sixteen. She still insisted on us remaining tight. For a while it even worked. But I wasn't honest with myself. Seeing Sam with his arm around Pamela, giggling at secrets behind their open lockers, did hurt.

And then, after Sam was well and truly ensnared, she moved on to someone else's boyfriend. That was the worst of it. I didn't think she even wanted Sam; she wanted him because he was mine.

That was what, twelve years ago? And I still felt the burn in my chest as though it was yesterday. I never gave my heart as openly or fearlessly again.

Betrayal is like that. It eats away long after the hurt's been done.

"What are you doing here?" I tried to keep my voice pleasant. This was my place of business, after all. "In Oxford."

She put her hands together under her chin. It was a mannerism that was so Pamela. Her nails were perfectly manicured, and I noticed her watch was a diamond-encrusted Cartier.

"I needed to get away after the horror of my divorce," she said as though we were still close. I didn't know she was married. Now she was divorced. "You must have heard."

I shook my head. "No. I hadn't heard that. I'm sorry." I really didn't follow her movements. I assiduously avoided any contact with her on social media, and none of my close friends ever bothered to talk about her. In one way or another, she'd hurt or infuriated all of us. If we ever wanted to describe someone loathsome, all we had to say was one word. *Pamela.* And then everybody got it.

"I'm a student here. I'm doing a master's degree in the history of art, at Cardinal College. I can't believe no one told you." Right. Because Pamela was the center of the universe, of course I should be aware of all her actions.

Me with my two years of college and Pamela was taking a master's at Oxford. Was I jealous? Maybe I felt a quick, sharp pang of envy, but it was followed by a creeping sense of horror. Cardinal College was only a short walk from here. She pretended to be thrilled. "I can't believe we're neighbors."

My smile was unenthusiastic. The school terms in Oxford began in October. It was now halfway through April, and Trinity term would begin next week. She'd been here months and hadn't bothered to stop by (which was fine by me). Why the sudden interest?

"And look at your little shop," she said, turning in a full circle to scan the shelves of wool, the ready-made sweaters that were in endless supply thanks to the vampire knitting club, the magazines and books and the knitting-related pictures on the walls. "It's so sweet."

She could try and belittle me with her poison dressed as honey, but I was older now and mostly immune. So I treated her the way I would an enemy in my shop. Perhaps someone I suspected of shoplifting and wanted out. "Do you knit?"

As if. Unless it was knitting up trouble. Knotting people's emotions. Crocheting an emotional crisis. I could go on and on with my knitting metaphors. The point was, she was bad news. And I didn't want bad news here. I'd have to cleanse the space once she'd gone.

She laughed. I had a feeling she'd been working on that laugh. I never remembered it being so silvery and charming. I thought when she'd been younger it was like the sound a horse makes when it gets close to feeding time. "No. I'm only here because I heard my dearest friend from the old days was in Oxford as well. I wanted to come by and say hello. And to invite you to a little party I'm having."

If Pamela, with her designer clothes and fancy watch, was inviting me to a party, there was an ulterior motive.

I might not be the sharpest knitting needle in the shop, but I wasn't a naïve sixteen-year-old anymore either. "What kind of party?"

"Just a few friends." I couldn't imagine what she wanted me for.

I was about to refuse as politely as I could when William Thresher walked into the shop. William was Rafe Crosyer's butler, his estate manager, I suppose you'd call him. William's passion was cooking. Since Rafe, being a vampire, obviously didn't put much strain on William's culinary talents, William had started catering events. Word had quickly spread, and he was so popular that he'd become very choosy. He particularly liked weddings.

It was a bit sad, because William was in his thirties and, according to his destiny, the first son he sired would be groomed and trained to serve Rafe when he came of age and William got old enough to retire. This pattern had remained unbroken since the first William Thresher served Rafe back in the 1500s. But how many appropriate women did William meet living in a grand estate run by a vampire? The answer was very, very few. To meet a woman with a strong pulse, he really needed to get out more. I'd been quite hopeful that the catering would encourage him to find someone nice. I wasn't entirely sure how I felt about him fathering Rafe's next servant, but it wasn't my business. Nobody had forced William into the job, and nobody could promise that the next William Thresher, assuming there was a next William Thresher, would grow up and want to serve Rafe.

Maybe he'd want to be a firefighter, a cop or a race-car driver. In my meaner moments, I hoped the next William Thresher chose any profession but butler to Rafe Crosyer, who had altogether too many advantages as it was.

Far be it from me to interfere with destiny, though. Especially since I'd discovered that I was a witch and part of a long tradition of witches here in Oxford. If I knew anything about destiny, it was that you can't escape yours.

Pamela brightened immediately when she saw William. When I looked at him dispassionately, I could see that William was a nice-looking man. Usually when I saw him, he was with Rafe, and it was like trying to admire the moon when it was beside the sun. But on its own, the moon was very handsome. He clearly noticed Pamela and gave her a shy nod.

"Lucy," he said, "I wanted to talk to you about something. But I can come back later."

"That's all right. I've got some time." I turned to Pamela with what I hoped was an "it's time for you to leave now" expression on my face. "Thanks for dropping by."

She ignored me and stared at the new arrival. "Aren't you William Thresher?"

I don't know who was more surprised, William or me,

that she knew who he was. He wasn't a movie star or a rock star or a media personality. He looked quite startled. Glanced at me as though I might know how she knew him, but I shrugged my shoulders. Finally, he answered, "Yes. I am."

"I thought it was you." She turned on the charm. And when Pamela turned on the charm, it was quite something. Even I, who distrusted and frankly loathed her, felt the warmth in her smile. "You're surprised I even know who you are. But you're a wizard in the kitchen. I was hoping you might cater a small party I'm having. I was just asking Lucy here to come by. We're old friends, you know, from America."

"I caught the accent, yes." He looked so pleased for me. "Lucy, how nice for you to have a friend from home. I know you get homesick sometimes."

So not homesick for Pamela.

"Well, I don't do very many private parties. It would depend on the date and the kind of party it is. But, since you're Lucy's friend—"

And boom. There it was. The reason Pamela had sought me out. She must have discovered that William was the best caterer in Oxford and, somehow, that I knew him.

She laughed and made a sort of fluttering motion with her hands. "In truth, the party's for my professor. I'm an art history student, you know. He's having a book published by Oxford University Press. And I wanted to organize a little shindig. Of course, I'm only going to be a waitress there myself. I was hoping that Lucy might help me out and be another server."

Ha. I'd known there was some backstabbing trick embedded in her quote, unquote invitation.

"Really?" William looked delighted. "Have you got much waitressing experience?"

What? How was this conversation getting so skewed? The only kind of serving Pamela knew how to do was to serve her own interests. I suddenly knew why William was here, and I did not want Pamela having any part of it.

"I'm sure Pamela's not interested in being a waitress," I said. Then turned to her. "Listen, Pam, I'll call you." I didn't know how much more obvious I could be that I wanted to get rid of the woman, but she remained oblivious to my broad hints.

She pretty much talked over my shoulder to William as though I wasn't even there. "I've done a lot of waitressing." (Not true.) "I had to save up the money to be able to afford Oxford." (So not true.) "But if you want something badly enough, it's worth waiting for." She laughed again, that pretty, silvery laugh. "You probably won't believe it, but I'm as old as Lucy."

Oh, and thanks for that.

William not only missed the jab at me, he looked delighted. "This is brilliant. I came here to ask Lucy if she could help me out by being a server at a private catered function. I could use another experienced server, if you're interested. It's all very secret, and you'd have to sign a nondisclosure agreement."

I felt a vague alarm. Somehow, without any provocation whatsoever, Pamela had managed to inveigle herself once more into my life. Because of course, I wasn't going to turn down this waitressing gig. I knew exactly what he was talking about. The members of the Gargoyle Club had a special annual dinner coming up for St. George's Day. Rafe had told me all about it. However, since the current crop of Gargoyles had caused so much trouble, local restaurants were closed to them. Rafe and some of the older members had decided to keep an eye on them, so they were having a private, catered dinner in one of the parents' homes—a man who had himself been a Gargoyle. That was all I knew.

Naturally, William had been asked to cater. And it was a brilliant idea, getting me to be one of the servers at the very secret dining club.

But why Pamela?

I tried to stand behind her and shake my head urgently at William, but he was dazzled by her charm, drawn into her web, as everybody was when they first met her. It was only when they'd been choked by silk threads and sucked dry of any life that they realized what she'd done. By then it was too late.

"Wonderful," she said as though the epitome of her ambition was to be a waitress at a private party. She reached out to shake William's hand. "I'm Pamela Forbes."

"Forbes?" I asked. Everything had tipped sideways since she walked in.

She looked at me as though I was thicker than my chunkiest wool. "My married name. I married Conrad Forbes. Sadly, we're divorced now." She looked down as though she couldn't bear to think of the tragedy. Conrad Forbes was a name I knew. He was a huge property developer in Boston. He'd inherited the company, and a fortune, from his father and continued to increase it. Pamela had married well.

And why was she stooping to be a waitress anyway? Pamela craved the high life. She'd started social climbing

11

before most of us were old enough to know what it was. Something was wrong here.

Naturally, because I so didn't want her to take the job, Pamela immediately agreed. She got out her phone and ostentatiously put the date in her "The world revolves around Pamela" app.

"The location's secret. So the best thing is if we meet here at Lucy's shop this Thursday at five forty-five p.m. I'll drive you both in the van."

It didn't seem to occur to either of them that he hadn't asked me, and I hadn't accepted. However, there was no way Pamela was going to be cozying up to William without me there to supervise. William might be domestic help, but thanks to his family being connected with Rafe for so long, I suspected he was quietly very wealthy. One sniff of that, and Pamela would be wrapping herself around him like a Venus flytrap around an unsuspecting bluebottle.

She gave me a hug and a brilliant smile as she was leaving. "I'm so excited, Lucy. We'll be able to have a proper catch-up. I can't wait."

When she left, I turned on William. "What on earth made you offer her a job?"

He looked stunned at my outburst. "I thought she was your friend. And coming from the United States, she's very unlikely to cause any trouble here. One has to be so careful in Oxford. So many people know each other. And you know what those boys are. That's why we're catering. To make sure they don't get out of hand again."

"Rafe's going to be there?"

"That's right. A few of the older members are coming back for the evening, just to keep an eye on things."

"I don't trust Pamela. She's not a good person."

He looked like I'd cheated him in some way. "Well, then, why were you acting so friendly to her? Now look what you've made me do."

As he walked out of the shop, my mouth was hanging open. How was this my fault?

CHAPTER 2

The night of the dinner, Rafe surprised me by paying me a visit. He rang the intercom, and I let him into my flat above Cardinal Woolsey's. I'd be seeing him soon enough at the Gargoyle dinner, but we wouldn't be chatting other than me asking him if he'd like more gravy. In British social terms, he'd be upstairs and I'd be downstairs.

"Wow," I said, when he walked in. He was always effortlessly gorgeous, but dressed so fancy, he took my breath away. He wore a navy blue tailcoat, the tails of the jacket long at the back and the button-up part only slightly longer than the cream silk waistcoat. The jacket had silk lapels and a velvet collar. His crisp white dress shirt was finished off with a maroon-colored bow tie. "Is this left over from when you used to party with Dickens?" I had to ask. All he needed was the top hat and cane, and he could walk straight out of my shop and into *Great Expectations*.

His eyes glinted as he gazed down at me. "Certainly not. This, my pretty innocent, is the uniform of the Gargoyle Club."

I was astonished. "You mean ordinary mortals wear that getup? Today?"

"Yes."

The brass buttons had a curious embellishment on them. I looked closer. "What's that? Your royal coat of arms?" Oh, and he had one. William showed it to me once.

"It's a simplified version of the Order of the Garter. You see, Henry Somerset, Duke of Beaufort, was the one who started the club. He was a Garter Knight, and this insignia is a nod both to the Order of the Garter and to his own coat of arms."

"I have a handbag that says Gucci on it." I got it second-hand, and I suspected it was a knockoff to begin with.

He didn't rise to the bait. He changed the subject. "You look nice."

I made a face. I had my long, blond hair tied up in a bun to keep it out of the way. And I was dressed in proper serving attire. White blouse and a black skirt. William's orders. For such an easygoing guy, William was very particular when it came to his catering jobs.

This wasn't the first time I'd helped him out by waitressing. I found it fun, I made a bit of extra pocket money, and since I was out front serving, I kept my eye open for the next Mrs. William Thresher.

I wouldn't find any candidates for the role of William's wife tonight, however, since this was an all-male club. But Rafe was part of the secret order, and I'd heard such scandalous stories that I was intrigued.

"Is it true that most of the political elite of Britain and sons of half the titled families belonged to that club?"

"The press does like to blow things out of proportion," he

said, sounding disgusted with everything to do with Fleet Street.

So not an answer. "So it's true then?"

"Lucy. Henry Somerset was a soldier, and he was cricket mad. It was simply a place for young and well-connected gentlemen to enjoy sporting events and then gather for a very nice dinner and discuss politics. And perhaps to make those lifelong connections that would be so important going forward. Over time, I admit, a certain rowdiness and licentiousness entered into the proceedings. Yes, simply because a disproportionate number of prime ministers and members of the royalty have gone to Oxford, there have been a number of very influential people who were also Gargoyles."

He could make it sound like they were serious young men discussing Plato and the Boer War, but I'd done a little digging of my own. "I read that their bad behavior was legendary. Many a restaurant owner has been heavily bribed to keep quiet. And many a tradesman's daughter."

He looked as though he tasted something bad. "Not tonight. This is a very special evening. It's St. George's Day. This is when we gather to celebrate the feast of St. George, patron saint of England and also the patron saint of the Knights of the Garter."

This sounded like something out of a fantasy. "The Knights of the Garter? Are they something to do with the Knights of the Round Table?"

He got this look when I said something ridiculous. He didn't actually roll his eyes, but there was a shifting of the eyeballs that suggested he would have rolled them if he could have been bothered. "The Most Noble Order of the Garter is an extremely old order, Lucy. It began in 1348 under King

Edward III, and to this day the order continues. There can only ever be twenty-four Knights of the Garter at one time. The ruling monarch and the heir to the throne are automatic knights, and the rest are appointed."

"Are there any young, hot ones?" I was thinking, of course, of Lancelot and Sir Galahad.

Once more he did that not quite eye rolling thing. "I don't believe there's a single knight under sixty. And twenty of the twenty-four are in their eighties or nineties."

Not a bunch of hotties then.

"However, other than Henry, several Gargoyles have gone on to become Knights of the Garter. So it has particular significance to our club. That's the ostensible reason why several of the older members will be going tonight. We'll get together with the current members, have a toast and a few words, and then we'll go upstairs for our quiet dinner and let them get on with theirs."

"And I'll be serving them."

"Exactly."

He shifted a little from one foot to the other. For a man who was usually so still, it was jarring, as though he were jumping up and down and doing jumping jacks in his tuxedo. "Officially, the Gargoyles have disbanded. As all secret societies have been banned from Oxford university campuses."

"For good behavior?" I asked, feeling cheeky.

He ignored my interruption. "The recent vandalism and general vile behavior do not reflect our values. There's a continuity and a history that should not be broken. So I'm asking you and William to keep an eye on things. William says he's also engaged a friend of yours from America. They'll be under a parental roof, but I still felt it was best to have eyes

17

and ears in the dining room to prevent any unfortunate behavior."

Was I hired to be a waitress or a spy? "What do we do if things get out of hand?"

He looked at me. "You have certain powers that could come in very handy."

"You want to put good behavior spells on them?" I wish I knew one. I'd use it on Pamela.

His lips quirked at that. "If necessary. And if you have the skill."

That was a low blow. I was a beginner witch, and I didn't have great control of my magic. I was taking lessons from the most annoying witch in the world, named Margaret Twigg, who loved to point out my deficiencies and make me feel stupid even as she was teaching me to get better.

"Call me if you need to. At the first sign of trouble. We can't have another incident getting into the newspaper. The reason we've had to do a catered dinner in a private home is that in recent years, the Gargoyles have destroyed so many restaurants and caused so much vandalism that no restaurateur wants them anymore. Even if they can get a reservation, which they have to do under a false name, the bad press isn't worth it." Of course, I remembered looking at the Oxford paper over Rafe's shoulder and seeing the article about vandalism caused by this supposedly secret society. Their name had to be part of the problem. Maybe when they started this club, they should have called it The Rosebuds or The Puppy Dogs. Gargoyles? I pictured all the terrifying monsters that leered in stone from all around Oxford. The boys were only living up to their club's name.

"Are you sure it's such a good idea to continue with this

thing? If they're so horrendously badly behaved that they keep breaking things and causing trouble, maybe the society should disband. You know, Rafe, things have changed a bit since you were young, five hundred years ago."

He shook his head at me. "People haven't changed, Lucy, not so much. What's changed is how very nosy people are. In the old days, there was more privacy. None of this social media." He said the words social media the same way you'd say social disease.

For a moment, I indulged myself in what Rafe's Twitter account might look like. Or what he might post on Instagram. Of course, being a vampire, he didn't turn out in pictures, so no endless selfies for him.

He looked momentarily uncomfortable. "I wasn't sure about having you do this. But I'll only be upstairs. If there's any problem, all you have to do is call out."

"If anybody tries anything with me, they'll be sorry." I said it all tough guy, but in reality, I wasn't entirely sure about my spells. I had protection spells and a few that would stop aggression. I wished one more time that Pamela wasn't going to be there. She wasn't a witch. Maybe she wasn't a very nice person, but I wouldn't wish her to get tangled up in something ugly because some entitled, rich boys got so drunk they started causing havoc.

Fortunately, William had also invited my cousin Violet, also a witch, to be a waitress. I figured two witches and one self-serving narcissist could handle a bunch of rowdy boys who drank too much. I was sure of it.

"I'll see you there, then," Rafe said. He touched my shoulder. "Remember. Call out, and I'll be by your side within a minute." It might sound like an idle boast, but with Rafe, I knew that was true. More than once I'd barely even let out a squeak and found him right beside me. One of his super-powers as a vampire. Still, I was sure I wouldn't need the help. I bid him goodbye and then made sure there was plenty of food for Nyx, who was out. Luckily for Rafe. Otherwise she'd have shown him so much affection, he'd currently have cat hair all over that fancy suit.

We were meeting at the shop, so I turned out the lights and walked down the stairs that led directly to the shop. Only a few minutes later, William came in. "You look nice, Lucy."

"I dressed exactly the way you asked me to. White blouse, black skirt."

"Well, you still look nice."

I smiled at him. "Thanks. So do you." He had a suit on, which was strange since he was the caterer, not the butler, tonight.

He saw my obvious confusion and explained that he'd be serving the wine. "I'll swap my apron for my suit jacket a few times. Nothing simpler."

Violet came in next. She'd taken the black and white thing slightly less traditionally. Her heart had recently been broken, but she must be feeling better about herself because she had dyed a purple and pink stripe down her long, black hair. She wore baggy cocktail pants in black, and her idea of a white blouse was an embroidered peasant blouse.

Then Pamela made her entrance. She walked in and stopped, like a runway model ready to be admired. There was a moment when we all said nothing. She wore high, black heels. That was the first thing I noticed. What kind of wait-ress wore high heels? They were patent leather and cut away, revealing beautifully manicured toes painted red. Her legs were excellent, and she showed them off with a figure-hugging skirt. Her blouse had to be pure silk based on the sheen, and it was low-cut. Her hair had clearly been freshly done at a salon, and her makeup was impeccable. Diamonds glinted from her ears.

William nearly swallowed his tongue. "Pamela. Pamela," he said again. "You look amazing." She laughed, that silvery laugh that was as fake as the spectacular cleavage she never had when I knew her.

Ouch, that was catty and unworthy of me. Pamela brought out the worst in me.

Because I'd had such unkind thoughts, I tried to be nice. We were going to be working together all evening, after all. "I hope you won't cripple yourself in those heels. I've got some flats upstairs if you want to borrow them."

Again with the silvery laugh. "I spend so much time in high heels that me wearing these would be like you wearing plaid bedroom slippers."

She's not insinuating you have no life. She's not. But I knew she was.

William had the nondisclosure agreements all ready, and we three signed them. He said, "Okay then. Let's go."

William ushered us out to his white van, which was waiting out front. Violet rode up front, and Pamela and I got into the back. The minute I got inside the van, my mouth started to water. "William, what have you got back there? It smells amazing."

He glanced at me in the rearview mirror, and his eyes crinkled. "I'm so glad you think so, Lucy. I admit, I put a lot of effort into this one. These young men will one day run this country. If I can impress them now, who knows where that could lead? Since it's St. George's Day, I stayed with British produce, local where I could get it."

Beside me, I felt Pamela perk up, and I didn't think she was interested in local produce. "Who's going to be there tonight?"

William didn't know Pamela the way I did. I'd probably have said I didn't know, which was true, but William was still under the spell of Pamela's charm. I wondered how long that would last. "Remember, you've signed an NDA," he reminded her.

She nodded, and he continued, "These young men are all part of the Gargoyle Club. It was originally a sports club, but it grew quite quickly into a dinner and debating club."

"Gargoyles? That's a funny name for a club. Aren't they basically fancy waterspouts?"

"You're quite right, Pamela," he said approvingly. "Their function is to divert rainwater from the roof to avoid the water ruining the stone of the cathedral or bank or whatever building the gargoyle adorns. However, they were also designed to frighten away evil. So, while they may look frightening, they're actually protecting people. That's why they face outward and are so often found on churches."

Appearances can be deceiving. I knew this as well as anyone. Witches were also often drawn as frightening hags, but the ones I knew used their powers for good. Of course, Margaret Twigg did look more than a little frightening, and I wasn't a hundred percent certain she was always a force for good.

"Who are these movers and shakers of the future?" Violet asked.

"I don't know. I only know that tonight's dinner will be held at the home of Sir Hugo Percival Brown."

Violet turned to him, and her mouth gaped. "The one from television?"

Sir Hugo Percival Brown was probably second to Richard Branson in wealth and fame as a British entrepreneur. He'd inherited a newspaper empire from his grandfather and branched out into all kinds of businesses. Now he was a celebrity businessman with companies ranging from grocery stores to media and airlines. He and his wife gave generously to charity, and he was often interviewed on TV about business affairs. He was a good talking head—nice-looking, intelligent and witty. He could explain complex business matters so people like me understood them. If I recalled correctly from things I'd read in newspapers and online, he had homes and business interests all over the world.

"His son, Teddy, is in the Gargoyles. Hugo was too, back in the day. But now that the boys have had some bad press lately, which they've richly deserved, Dad and some of his cronies have decided to bring the party under the parental roof. He and some of his friends will be having dinner upstairs, while the current members of the club will be in the main dining room."

"So we're catering two dinners," Pamela said.

William made a back and forth motion with his hand. "One dinner, served in two locations. That's right. But I think with the three of you, we'll be able to handle it."

I appreciated his confidence, but we weren't the most experienced of servers. I'd waitressed in a private club back in Boston for a couple of summers. Violet said she'd worked in a pub for a while. If Pamela had ever served anyone but herself, this was the first I'd heard of it. We'd make it work for William's sake. I wanted him to succeed probably as much as he did.

Pamela turned and gave me an intimate smile. If I didn't know better, I'd have thought we were still best friends. "It's exciting, isn't it? I wonder if we'll recognize any of them. So much gorgeous, British bachelordom. I can hardly stand it."

"We're there to serve them food," I reminded her somewhat tartly.

"Of course, but a girl can look, can't she?"

So long as she did nothing but look.

I still couldn't believe she'd managed to wangle her way into this. I'd bet there were people who had actual waitressing experience that would have been a much better fit.

We drove for about thirty minutes west of Oxford, which put us well into the Cotswold countryside. William took a smaller road, and I lost track of exactly where we were. We followed a high stone wall and then turned into a private drive. I peered eagerly out the window and saw trees, well-kept lawns, a stream with an ancient bridge crossing it. And then we rounded a corner, and the manor house lay ahead of us.

I'd pretty much guessed that a man as wealthy as Hugo Percival Brown wouldn't live in a shack, but the manor house still took my breath away. Made of the local stone, it was grand and sprawling. I'd lived in Oxford long enough that I could take a guess that it was originally Tudor but had been added to over the centuries. There were no other houses anywhere in sight, so they must own all these surrounding fields. I could see sheep grazing in the distance.

The catering van passed the grand entrance, and we

made our way around the side of the manor on a crushed gravel drive. We passed outbuildings, probably things like a dower house and old coach house. In the distance were paddocks and barns. We pulled up by a thick oak door and William said, "Right. Let's get the van unloaded and get to work."

We piled out of the van, and I noticed we were in front of a walled kitchen garden containing fruit trees in full blossom, and the air was perfumed with the scent of herbs. I'd have loved to poke around in there and see what they had, as I was beginning to learn about herbs, but there was no time for witch studies. I had to cater to a dining room full of destructive spoiled brats.

CHAPTER 3

William knocked on the kitchen door, and it was answered by a butler. Kind of ironic, since William usually did that at Rafe's equally impressive manor house. After a couple of minutes of conversation, he came back out, and the four of us carried in the trays and covered dishes from the back of the van.

I'd made sure to have a good meal about five, but even so, the smell of this food was nearly making me faint.

We were in a well-lit corridor with rooms opening off of it. One housed laundry; another looked to contain nothing but outdoor coats and shoes. There was a full bathroom, and then we entered the kitchen. The manor might be ancient, but this kitchen was sleek and modern and built for catering to crowds. Phew.

There were two gas ovens, industrial-size fridges, acres of marble countertop, two dishwashers and, in an alcove in front of a window, a kitchen table and chairs and a couple of cozy armchairs. No doubt the household staff took their meals here. I wondered what had happened to the old basement kitchens.

We stacked all the food on the counters, and the butler introduced himself as Jack Briggs. He was probably in his fifties, not at all stuffy, more like someone eager to please. He had a wide smile and begged William to save him some leftovers "because it smells amazing. My wife's the cook, and she turns out a lovely meal, but I'd still be very grateful if there was a plate left at the end of the evening."

The way to William's heart was through his food, so I knew Jack Briggs was going to get a very nice plate of leftovers.

"I'll be welcoming the guests at the front door, and then Hugo and Mrs. Percival Brown have kindly given me the night off." I thought that was strange. Who gave their butler a holiday on the night they were entertaining? Unless they didn't want someone local, who might be liable to gossip, witnessing whatever happened here tonight.

"Now, let me show you the principal rooms you'll be using."

We all nodded and followed. "This is the preparation room," he announced, leading us into a room off the kitchen that looked almost like a second kitchen, with the same granite countertops, double sinks and a wine fridge.

William said, "The food will be cooked and prepared in the kitchen and then brought in here, where you will take it into the dining room."

"Which is through here," Jack Briggs said, smoothly leading us into a sumptuous dining room. Sumptuous isn't a word I use very often, but it fit. The dining room was like something out of a movie set. Or a castle. It was gorgeous. The walls were painted in a dark maroon, which should have been hideous but wasn't, probably because of the quality of the art on the walls. Not that I knew much about art, but these were beautiful. From oil paintings of fields with horses in them and an oil that looked very old and featured the Madonna and child to a modern portrait with the face so lumpy-looking, I was certain it was a Lucian Freud.

Pamela headed straight for the Madonna and seemed to fall into a trance. "Is this a Bellini?" she asked, almost in a whisper.

"Yes. Well done. My employers love their art."

"This is exquisite." She looked over at me. "And of course that one, Lucy, is painted by Lucian Freud. His style is so unique."

Thank you Ms. Master of Art History, I'd worked that out for myself. Still, Bellini. I'd seen a few in places like The Louvre. I doubted his art collection rivaled Rafe's, but then Hugo Percival Brown only had one lifetime in which to do his collecting, so it wasn't fair to compare.

Enormous sideboards in rich woods gleamed with a fresh polishing. The chandelier looked priceless and extremely well polished, and it cast a fountain of light down on a long table perfectly set for twelve. I checked the gleaming silverware. Honestly, somebody must have used a ruler to get them so lined up. The napkins were crisp, perfectly folded. Wineglasses fanned out and glittered to their crystal depths.

There was nothing to do but light the candles.

"I'll show you a few other key rooms," Jack Briggs said, walking out of the room, and we followed as though we were tourists. I think we were all gazing about like tourists, too. I mean, we were inside Hugo Percival Brown's English manor house. Of course, we gawped. I knew he had a compound in the British Virgin Islands and homes in other parts of the world too.

Hugo Percival Brown was a seriously rich dude, and his home reflected that. As we walked down the hallway, we passed exquisite antiques, paintings that looked like they should hang in the National Gallery, mixed with informal family photos. I paused at a family grouping. There was, unmistakably, Hugo, and beside him was a thin, glamorous blond woman. Standing on either side of their parents were two really beautiful teenagers. One male, one female.

We paused when Jack did. In a soft voice, he said, "This is the main drawing room." I peeked inside and glimpsed Rafe and Hugo sharing a cocktail with two other men. All exuded wealth and power and somehow managed to not look like they were playing dress-up in their fancy suits.

A fire burned in the large fireplace. Two modern-looking couches faced each other in a cozy seating area in front of the fire. The rest of the furniture was a combination of designer originals and probably designer antiques. More remarkable art hung on the walls.

I knew Rafe could sense me there, but he didn't glance my way.

We passed the open doorway as though they were part of the exhibit, and then the butler took us up a wide staircase. "Mr. Percival Brown keeps a set of rooms and a second, smaller dining room up here, purely for business."

That seemed odd to me. One dining room for your friends and another for your business associates? Whatever. This dining room was smaller and much more modern. The table was glass, and the art was modern. An Andy Warhol I recognized. The brilliantly colored fields I thought was a David Hockney. Pamela barely listened to our instructions. She was walking around the room staring at each painting as though there'd be an exam at the end.

The table was set for four, and behind this dining room was another preparation kitchen.

We retraced our steps even though I'd have loved to tour the rest of this gorgeous home. Once back on the main level, Jack Briggs pointed out a door that I'd have missed. He opened it and gestured down another flight of stairs. "That leads to the games room, cinema and the wine cellar, should you need it."

From the amount of wine I'd spied in the wine fridges, I couldn't imagine there'd be a need.

The front doorbell went, and Jack Briggs waved his hands at us, motioning us to return to the kitchen. Not until we were out of sight did I hear him open the door.

Back in the kitchen, William took off his suit jacket and placed it on a handy hanger. No doubt Jack Briggs was accustomed to slipping his jacket on and off as well. He donned his big apron and went into catering mode. The man who was normally so deferential and soft-spoken turned into an efficient kitchen commander. I loved watching him switch like this. And I went from pampered guest and close friend to worker bee.

He set timers, and we helped him unpack all the food and put it where he told us to. Fridge or countertop. Nothing went in the oven yet, but William turned the ovens on.

He checked his watch. "Right. We've got thirty minutes until we serve the first course. Lucy, go into the dining room and check that the table is set correctly." He ran through the various forks and spoons and glasses, and I tried to memorize it all. "Mrs. Briggs was to set the table to my specifications, but I'd like you to double check."

I nodded, really hoping that Mrs. Briggs had done the job right because William had lost me at seafood fork (not to be confused with fish fork!).

"Violet, you do the same upstairs."

"I'll check the drawing room, see if drinks need freshening," Pamela said, clicking out on those ridiculous heels before William could stop her. As I watched her go, it occurred to me that she hadn't dressed for downstairs. She was groomed and gowned for upstairs.

I didn't need to do much in the dining room. Mrs. Briggs had done a better job than I would have, and everything seemed to be in its place, including a fan of wine glasses, each for a different kind of wine.

Back in the kitchen, William was working quickly and efficiently. He had the oven on, and the chafing dishes he'd brought were already set up.

Whenever the front doorbell rang, it rang in the kitchen, too, presumably so if the butler was back here, he could hotfoot it out front.

"When do you want me to light the candles in the dining room?"

He checked his watch. "At seven twenty-five, they'll all go into the dining room, where we'll serve the first appetizers and champagne." I could spend the rest of my life in that one room. It was so gorgeous.

I could hear the front doorbell ring and, obviously, the butler was answering the door. Meanwhile, I helped William plate the first course. It was four perfect and tiny morsels. A tiny tower of beetroot and smoked salmon, an oyster in its shell with some kind of sauce, a bit of roast duck served on a tiny potato rosti with feathers of fried onion, and a sliver of Melton Mowbray pork pie. "They'll be full before they get to the first course," I said.

"They're young lads with ferocious appetites. Anyway, the more I can get them to eat, the more it will soak up the alcohol." We carried the prepared plates into the preparation room.

William went to the big wine fridge and opened it. "When they first sit down, I'll open and pour champagne." He pulled out a bottle and gave a low whistle when he studied the label.

I looked over his shoulder. I didn't know much about champagne. This one was Krug from 2004. "Fancy?" I asked.

"This stuff is a thousand quid a bottle. Each bottle is numbered." Figured. Back in my college days, we got excited about a kegger.

"You're a wine expert too?"

He shrugged. "I bought a couple of cases of this for Rafe. He likes to keep his cellar well stocked."

He glanced at his watch. "You can light the candles in the dining room now."

Before I headed through the door, he stopped me. "Lucy, these young men don't have the best reputations. Come and get me if there's any trouble at all."

"They're in a parent's house. How much trouble can they cause?"

He rolled his eyes. "From what I've heard, quite a bit. Just don't take any nonsense."

I was getting tired of these warnings. I wasn't a defenseless damsel in distress. "I have no intention of it."

I went through to the dining room. I had my back to the main doorway to the room, the one that led to the hallway that the guests used. I was leaning over lighting the candelabra in the middle of that beautiful, polished dining table when someone behind me said in a super posh voice, "Hello. I had no idea tonight's dinner was going to be quite so delectable."

Seriously?

I turned around and saw a gorgeous-looking guy leaning against the doorjamb with studied casualness. He was wearing the same outfit Rafe had on. The navy suit with big, embossed brass buttons, the cream silk waistcoat, maroon bow tie and highly polished shoes. He should have looked ridiculous, but he looked amazing, like one of the actors in a BBC period drama had stepped out of the screen and was talking to me. He had blond, wavy hair, chiseled features, deep and beautiful blue eyes. Also an I-could-eat-you-all-up grin. He couldn't have been more than twenty-one or -two, and he looked as though he owned the world. Of course, if he was in this club, he probably owned part of it.

I tried to send him a glance that said, "Don't mess with me, buddy" and added, "Sorry, I'm not on the menu."

His gaze traveled from the top of my head to the bottom of my shoes, taking their lazy time doing it too. "Maybe later then."

Maybe never. Before I could answer, three more guys came in. All wearing the same outfit and all equally gorgeous. It was like these boys had been taken as babies, polished, given every possible advantage from the best food to the most amazing cultural enrichment and sheltered from every ill wind. They looked like they'd never suffered a pimple, a cold, a bad day at school or a broken heart. I suppose there was a kind of natural selection in rich, powerful people marrying connected, beautiful people. Over time they turned out these exceptionally gorgeous, talented and entitled Oxford undergrads.

The only thing that was missing in their lives was hardship. Or maybe I was being judgmental and unfair. Their lives were probably no easier than anybody else's. While Oxford was tough to get into, if anybody ever had a path to that ancient, prestigious door, it was each one of these young men standing in front of me.

"Lucy, is that you?"

I glanced up as a fifth member of the Gargoyles walked in. He fit right in, with that casual nonchalance, even while wearing the club uniform that, according to William, cost nearly four thousand pounds. Still, I was delighted to see the guy looking at me with a cocky grin. He came forward for a hug, and I was pleased to wrap my arms around him.

"Miles Thompson. Whatever are you doing here?" Stupid question since he was obviously in the club. Miles had been one of the actors in the rather unfortunate production of *A Midsummer Night's Dream* that Cardinal College had put on last year. At one point, I'd even suspected him of murder, when he'd only been guilty of sleeping with a former A-list actress and the play's director, Ellen Barrymore.

"I'm here to celebrate St. George's Day, of course. England's patron saint that celebrated slayer of dragons." He was such a great actor. He sounded like he was on the stage spouting Shakespeare. "And what brings you into our midst?"

"I'll be your server tonight," I told him. I acted as though this were one of those dining places in the States where everybody knows your name. "My name's Lucy, if you need anything."

"Like a leg over," said the rude guy who'd already suggested I might be on the menu. And they hadn't even had their first glass of champagne. I had an inkling I'd be earning my wages tonight.

"Stop it, Charles." Miles shook his head at me, looking a bit embarrassed by his fellow Gargoyle. He turned to the far too cute guy still holding up part of the doorway. "Charles Smythe-Richards, meet Lucy Swift. Lucy's a friend of mine who runs a knitting shop in Oxford. I assume that's still true?"

"Yes. The caterer's a friend. I help him sometimes."

Charles Smythe-Richards did not look particularly concerned one way or the other what I might do with any part of my time that didn't involve him. He merely nodded and once more did that insolent, slow gaze from the top of my head to the bottom of my feet. I wondered if he had any other way of communicating with women. Given how cute he was, he probably didn't have to try very hard. Miles took my arm and pulled me gently toward the window, where we could speak without being overheard. "I'm sorry to find you here, Lucy. These are good mates of mine, but get a few drinks into them, and they can get carried away."

I was a little disappointed that Miles would want to be part of this club. "What are you even doing here? I thought you only had time for acting."

He made a face. "After what happened, you know, during *A Midsummer Night's Dream,* my father put his foot down. No more acting for me."

I couldn't believe it. "But you're an amazing actor. Ellen

Barrymore might have been psycho, but she was right about your talent. You could be the next Olivier or Aidan Turner."

"I know," he agreed, looking frustrated and sad. "And it was all right within my grasp." He held out his hand, cupped, to demonstrate. "But when Father's goodwill dries up, so does the money." He shook his head. "Oh, don't worry, I've still got every intention of pursuing theater. But, for now, I pretend I'm willing to go into the family business."

"What is his problem?" I asked, glancing at Charles Smythe-Richards, who was still checking me out.

"His problem is he thinks the sun shines out of his arse. His mother's a cabinet minister, his father is high up in the City, and everything's always come easy to him. He's not a bad guy, really, but if he makes a pass at you, I wouldn't take him up on it."

"Don't worry."

Another young man came in. He was tall with strawberry-blond hair and rather protuberant, blue eyes.

Miles followed my gaze. "That's Alexander Percival Brown. He's the son of—"

"Don't tell me. Let me guess. Hugo Percival Brown?"

"That's right. Alex is definitely the richest one here. Dolph over there, that's Lord Randolph Chase, the chubby, shy one. He's the most posh. His mother or grandmother was a lady-in-waiting to the queen, I think." Now that he'd begun, he told me about the rest of them. "Winnie, that's Winston Bromford. He's the dark-haired fellow over there. His family owns Bromford Chemists." I knew that chemists were drugstores and you'd find a Bromford's on just about every high street in every town in England.

"The shorter, dark-haired bloke is Gabriel Parkinson. He's

half Colombian. His mother's family have emerald mines. She married a British engineer she met down there."

I turned to him, "And what about you? How do you fit in with this bunch?"

He looked sort of embarrassed. "Have you heard of Thompson Sugar?"

Only every morning when I poured it into my coffee. "You're that Thompson?"

"'Fraid so."

"Wow."

He looked embarrassed. "It's nothing I did. My great-great-grandfather created this sugar empire. We're still running the company. I'm expected to step into my father's shoes if he ever decides to retire." His voice began to lose its sparkle, and I thought how unfair I'd been. Sure, these guys were rich and privileged, but I bet all of them had their futures mapped out for them. Miles would be the next CEO of Thompson Sugar; that had been his destiny since birth. For him to become an actor was probably a pipe dream. I wondered if his dad was also behind him belonging to the Gargoyles.

I might not have any money or have had the best education, but at least I'd always been free in my choices.

Then a truly beautiful man with dark hair and flashing dark eyes came in. I think I stopped breathing for a moment. Miles caught the direction of my gaze and grinned. "Prince Vikram Singh, son of the Maharaja of Pune."

He called tall, dark and gorgeous over. "Hi there, Prince Vikram. Come and meet Lucy Swift."

Prince Charming walked over and punched Miles gently in the upper arm. "It's plain Vikram." He glanced around and leaned in, "Or Vickie when they get drunk enough." Then he extended his hand. "It's a pleasure to meet you, Lucy."

He acted as though I were an honored guest, so I hastened to explain. "I'll be one of the servers tonight."

"Then we will try to behave." His smile was as gorgeous as the rest of him, and he didn't seem remotely bothered that I was here to serve. I liked him instantly for being gorgeous and having good manners. Unlike his pervy friend Charles.

Rafe and Hugo Percival Brown came in next. Hugo had a very commanding way about him. A bit like Rafe. Two more men came in behind them. They were closer to Hugo's age and all wore the same uniform. One was tall, blond and gorgeous and about thirty-five, the other in his fifties, a bit chubby with a receding chin.

Rafe looked over and found me, and I excused myself and went to speak to him. He said, "It's probably time to bring out the champagne now. We'll all have the first courses together, and then the older members will go on upstairs while the younger members have the dining room to themselves."

I nodded, though William had briefed me. "I'll tell William we're almost ready if you get everyone to sit down."

I headed back to the kitchen. Pamela was just ahead of me, and I walked in right behind her. William glanced up at her. "There you are. Where have you been?"

"I was making sure the gentlemen had fresh cocktails, that's all."

He glared at her for a moment, but he didn't have time for more. He said, "I'll come in and pour the champagne. You two"—he pointed to me and Pamela—"put a plate in front of each guest. Violet, you watch the scallops. Any questions?"

We three shook our heads. "All right." He removed his

apron, unrolled his shirtsleeves and quickly donned the black jacket and was instantly transformed into the perfect maître d' and host. Impressive.

"Remember, even if it gets hectic, once you enter that dining room, you will smile, move without haste, and see that glasses remain filled." He'd already told us all this, but we all nodded once more. "Let's move."

Pam and I followed him into the prep room. He took two bottles of the expensive fizz, and we followed with the plates of food. The Gargoyles were all sitting at the table. They looked slightly stiff, but I could see they were ready to have a good time. Hugo Percival Brown sat at the head of the table and his son at the foot. The gorgeous blond man sat beside Hugo, and something about him made me look twice. For some reason he reminded me of Rafe. I didn't know why, because his hair was fair, not dark, and he looked more Nordic than British. It was a certain power that I felt coming from him. I looked at Rafe and back at him, and I realized he was a little on the pale side. I'd assumed he was from a cold climate, but now I began to wonder. Could he be a vampire?

CHAPTER 4

While William poured champagne, he described each of the morsels on the elegant china. "Everything tonight is British-grown and -sourced in honor of St. George's Day."

As we were walking out, Hugo rose to his feet, ready to propose a toast. I felt he was waiting for us to leave before he did so.

We went back to the kitchen, and William once again swapped his dinner jacket for his apron.

The first course was baked scallops on a pea puree with marinated mushrooms. They were served on scallop shells, so they had a whimsical look to them.

"Why scallops? That's not very British," I said.

"In fact, they are British scallops, Lucy. But St. George was never even in England. He was a bit of a pilgrim, so the scallop is a fanciful way of celebrating that."

"Really? They look good too." Also, they smelled divine. I was really hoping there would be some leftovers after this so that I could try some of these amazing dishes that

William had prepared. "Wait a minute. St. George, the patron saint of England, was never even in this country? Are you sure?"

"It's what Rafe says. We chose St. George because of his bravery and for defeating dragons."

"I'll remember that if I have to fight off any Gargoyles." Based on the pervy Charles, it was likely to happen.

This was to be a leisurely dinner, so William was waiting to serve each course until Hugo rang. That table might be a glorious antique, but there was a very high-tech communication system between the dining room and kitchen.

William went out twice more to refill champagne glasses before Pam and I were sent in to remove the first plates.

We removed the tiny appetizers and put the scallops in front of the dinner guests. I wasn't sure how Rafe would manage. I'd seen him eat small quantities of food to be polite, but no doubt he and William had something worked out between them.

I only heard snatches of conversation, and it all seemed to be Cardinal College politics and regular British politics. While the older men were there, I suspected the younger men were on their best behavior.

When we got to the scallops, William allowed me to open and pour the wine (another fancy French one—clearly the British menu didn't extend to the wines).

I was kept busy refilling glasses, and then we moved to the third course. Parsnip soup. Somehow, William had made the very pedestrian parsnip soup look, and smell, amazing. He'd drizzled it with a watercress reduction, and we moved on to a third wine, this one German.

Once the soup was done, the four older Gargoyles rose.

As Rafe and the tall blond guy stood, Rafe made a subtle motion with his chin for me to follow.

When the three of us were alone in the hall, he said, "How are you making out so far?"

"Yeah, great. I just wish I could sit down and eat some of this stuff. It smells amazing."

In a low voice, Rafe said, "A little richer than my usual diet." Right, I had to stop talking about food in front of him. His dietary needs were so different from mine.

The fact that he'd said the words in front of the blond man made me pretty sure my suspicions had been correct. He said, "Lucy, I'd like you to meet Lochlan Balfour. Lochlan lives in Ireland. He's a special guest tonight, as he's a Knight of the Garter. Though no one knows that, of course."

"I thought you were a Gargoyle?" I was getting so confused.

They both laughed a kind of superior har-har-har, and Rafe explained, "We are both Gargoyles. However, being a Knight of the Garter is an extremely high honor. The Order has been going since the thirteen hundreds and is bestowed by the monarch. St. George is closely associated with the Knights of the Garter. So it's a real honor for us to have Lochlan here tonight."

"You said the Knights of the Garter were a bunch of old guys."

The two kind of smirked at each other. Lochlan said, in a very low voice, "I am an old guy. I'm older than Rafe."

I looked at him, and his eyes were twinkling. Rafe was five hundred years old. How old could this guy be? I was seriously going to have to do a search on Google and see if I could find his name. Somewhere there must be lists of all the Knights of the Garter, because if I recalled correctly, there were only ever a maximum of twenty-four of them at one time.

It seemed like something Rafe would have done at some point in his career. "Were you ever a Knight of the Garter?" I asked him.

"No."

Lochlan shook his head when Rafe didn't elaborate. "You're too modest, Rafe." He turned to me. Clearly Rafe had told him that I could be trusted and knew all their secrets, for he said, "Queen Elizabeth, and I mean the first to bear that name, wanted to make Rafe a Knight of the Garter. And in my opinion, she should simply have done it. But she made the mistake of consulting Rafe, and he turned down the honor."

I was shocked. "You did? Who would turn down an honor like that from the queen herself?"

"Someone who didn't want to have a high profile. I had done some spying for the queen. If any of my secret activities became public, I didn't want anything to besmirch her fair name."

That was so sweet, I smiled at him. "Chivalry. I like that."

Lochlan shook his head. "Women. Seven hundred years I've been alive, and they haven't changed a bit."

For some reason, that didn't sound much like a compliment. I could hear Hugo's voice, wishing the younger men a good dinner. Rafe said, "We're adjourning upstairs now. You remember what I said. Call my name, and I'll hear you if you need anything. Anything at all."

"And so will I," added Lochlan Balfour. "I'm the true Knight of the Garter, after all."

"Braggart," Rafe replied.

I appreciated their protectiveness, but it seemed a little

over the top considering that we were in Hugo Percival Brown's home, not some pub where these guys could get away with murder. "I'll be fine."

Hugo and the fourth of the older Gargoyles joined us. "All right, gentlemen? Let's adjourn upstairs. And let the mayhem begin."

They went off, and I scurried back to the dining room to catch up on my duties. When I got there, I saw Pamela didn't seem to have done much in the way of clearing the plates and putting out the fresh ones. She was bending over, speaking to Alexander Percival Brown. He replied in a low voice. What on earth was she doing? Giving out her phone number?

"Pamela," I said, slightly sharply. "If you finish clearing the soup, I'll pour the next wine."

The glance she sent up at me under her lashes was not the friendliest. She didn't immediately move, and she might as well have shouted, *You are not the boss of me.*

William had already given me the rundown on the next wine course. This was the one we'd been working up to. The highlight of the evening. He had already opened a couple of bottles and had them decanted.

"What a beauty," he said, pouring a tiny bit into a glass, then swirling, sniffing and finally tasting it. Seeing me looking at him with eyebrows raised, he said, "Of course, 1995 was an excellent year for burgundies. This is a grand cru from Nuits-Saint-Georges." He poured a taster for me. I sipped it and thought it was very nice, but I doubted my budget would stretch this far. "Don't tell me, it's a thousand pounds a bottle too?"

He laughed softly. "Much, much more. Of course, Hugo Percival Brown would have bought the wine when it was first available and cellared it. Still, I bet he's got a fortune in wines in his cellar."

"He has his own wine cellar?" I thought the wine fridge was impressive.

"Yes. When we discussed the menu, we also planned the wines to go with each course. Wine's a hobby of his, so I expect his cellar is first-rate."

William always had one eye on the clock, and he nodded, pleased. "Good. Half past eight, and we're right on schedule." And then we brought in William's beef Wellington. It was a thing of beauty. Perfect browned pastry lined with both a mushroom duxelle and a layer of paté around a succulent beef filet. With it were potatoes, roasted with garlic and herbs, and baby carrots in butter and almonds.

Pam poured wine, and I served the beef Wellington. "Where's Jeremy?" I asked, noticing his chair was empty, napkin laid on the seat.

"He's gone for a fag. Just leave his dinner on the table. His fault if it's cold," Alex instructed. Jeremy had gone for a cigarette right before the main course was served? How rude.

I could feel that the atmosphere had changed the minute the older men had left the room. The young men were looser, joking with each other and sitting at their ease. Pam poured the rich, red wine into all the glasses, and as she was about to put the rest of the wine back in the prep area, Alex Percival Brown said, "No, no. Leave it on the table. And open a couple more, would you?"

When I thought of all the things even one bottle of this wine could buy, I was shocked, and they were just getting William to open bottles. I began to get an inkling of what it was like to live in this world. These guys were going to be hammered before they ever got to their potatoes.

I put Charles's dinner in front of him, and he slipped his hand under my skirt. He didn't change expression or move any part of his body but that wandering hand. I knew all I had to do was call out for Rafe, and I'd likely have the satisfaction of seeing Pervy Charles go crashing through the dining room window. But I wasn't without defenses all my own. In the olden days, naughty English schoolboys had to hold out their hands and they'd be caned. I'd seen it in an old movie.

I wasn't big on corporal punishment, but Charles needed a lesson. His hand was hot and squeezing. I pictured his palm held open, and in my mind I took a narrow cane and whacked the palm that was even now inching higher.

He let out a yelp of pain and dropped his hand away.

I moved smoothly out of range as Vikram asked, "Are you all right?"

He was staring at his open palm as though looking for the welt or a sting perhaps. There was nothing there. He shrugged, looking sulky. "The waitress trod on my foot."

Miles caught my gaze and gave the tiniest nod. No doubt he thought I had stepped on Charles's foot, and he probably knew why and approved my actions. Though the caning had been so much more satisfying. And, I thought, how typical of Charles to make it sound like I'd been clumsy instead of admitting that he'd been inappropriate.

William went to open more wine, and as Pam and I followed, Alex said, "Thank you. We'll ring the bell if you're wanted." Just as though I'd been some poor, overworked maid in Victorian times. It was everything I could do not to curtsy as I left the room.

I got the message loud and clear. *Stay out.*

Charles Smythe-Richards reached out and grabbed my arm. Some guys never learned. "Wait a minute. I need you." He turned to his host. "Why don't we get the girls to join us? They're all lovely. Add a bit of spice to this rather dull gathering."

Alex looked toward Pam as though he was considering extending the invitation, but Miles once more told Charles not to be so stupid. "We'll go out later. Then you can cause all the trouble you like. While we're here, remember, Lucy's my friend. Try to control yourself."

Charles let me go but replied to Miles, "I wouldn't boast about being friendly with the hired help."

Ass.

And speaking of asses. I pulled up my mental image of that cane again. Made it longer this time. Focused and... *Whack.*

"Agh," Charles cried, jumping up in his seat and frantically rubbing his backside.

With a serene smile, I walked out of the dining room.

I HEADED BACK to the kitchen, leaving them to it. I had helped William out a few times before, and I'd heard so many extravagant compliments about his glorious food that it hurt my feelings by proxy to have these boorish young men not have a single compliment for me to pass on to William.

I wondered if I should make a few up, but I knew I

wouldn't. He'd probably see right through me. In this instance, William was going to have to take pride in his own work, because I didn't think there were going to be any huge compliments thrown his way. Hopefully the men dining upstairs would have more class.

I'd barely reached the kitchen when Pamela said, "I'll see if they need anything upstairs."

William was getting the desserts ready. And they were beautiful. Since it was St. George's Day, he'd made tiny, perfect, round, steamed strawberry puddings with white marzipan making the cross of St. George. The belt was piped dark chocolate, and each had a tiny St. George's flag piped onto the center of the marzipan.

I didn't know if he knew that Lochlan Balfour was a genuine Knight of the Garter, but since William was more in Rafe's confidence than I was, no doubt he did. "These look amazing, William."

He looked quite pleased, as he should. This was his first genuine compliment of the evening.

"I hope they enjoy them."

"I hope they aren't too drunk to taste dessert." My disdain must have shown in my tone.

"Those young men will go on to great things one day. Let's hope they remember enough of my talents that they hire me one of these days. Or, better yet, Hugo and his wife do a lot of entertaining. One way or another, I'm sure something good will come of this."

I sidled up to him. "I'm hoping leftovers come out of this."

He chuckled. "Well, you've all certainly earned a good meal. If they really don't want to be bothered, you can tuck in. I've saved you some of everything."

Working for William wasn't about the hourly wage for me. Or even my share of the tips which, at a swanky do like this, ought to be pretty substantial. For me it was a chance to taste his amazing food. Plus, bonus! I was inside Hugo Percival Brown's house. Not many people could say that who didn't also see their names on the Fortune 500.

"Where's Pamela?" William asked, looking around.

"She said she was going to check on the other set of diners upstairs."

Violet said, "Where on earth did you dig her up from?"

"I knew her in Boston. We were high school friends."

Violet shook her head. "Well, you've got very peculiar taste in friends. And she's a useless waitress."

They were both looking at me like this was somehow my fault. I threw up my hands. "I never wanted her to come. I don't even like her."

"Well, I wish you'd said something before it was too late," Vi said. I wished she could have seen how hard I'd tried to stop William from offering Pam this waitressing job.

I was never going to win this argument, so I didn't bother having it. I was much more interested in trying some beef Wellington.

CHAPTER 5

We tucked in and gossiped and laughed in the kitchen. It was probably twenty minutes before any of us noticed that Pamela was still AWOL.

I suggested unenthusiastically that maybe I should go and look for her. Violet said, "Don't bother. I expect she left by the back door before anyone asked her to do the dishes."

I had other ideas. I strongly suspected that Pamela had used me to get inside this house. If I hadn't known her, maybe I wouldn't have suspected her of being so brazen, but I knew that where that woman had her eyes on a prize, she had no shame. But what was the prize? A peek at the Percival Brown private art collection?

I didn't think so.

Was she hoping to cozy up to one of these guys? Did she really think they were going to fall for a waitress at one of their drunken dinners?

As she had pointed out, we were the same age. At twenty-eight, she was already divorced from a rich husband. What, or whom, was she after now? And why the UK? Pamela was always focused on what Pamela wanted, but I was trying to figure out what that might be. Even more wealth? A title?

Not that I was particularly interested, but I thought when I got home, I might go online and check up on her. What had she been up to in the years since I'd last seen her? I wondered why she was really in Oxford because I seriously doubted it was the love of art history.

Another twenty minutes passed, and then William was so worried about his perfect desserts beginning to flop that he told me to check on the dinner club. See if Alex had simply forgotten to call us.

I made my way through the prep room and opened the door into the dining room. The guys were looking a lot the worse for wear. Most of them hadn't even eaten much of that fantastic dinner. But all the bottles of wine had now been drunk.

A couple of the diners were missing. Alex and Jeremy. Vikram was also missing. Maybe they'd gone to the bathroom. After all that wine, I wouldn't be a bit surprised.

"Lucy!" It was Miles looking blearily up at me. "We've missed you. Come and tell me all about the acting troupe. I miss them. Never wanted to give it up, you know."

"I only helped out with that one play, Miles. I don't know what they're doing."

I thought about it. "Anyway, wouldn't Sofia Bazzano know?" They'd been clearly an item during the time I'd known Miles. Sofia was a gorgeous girl. The last time I'd seen them, they'd been looking pretty cozy.

He waved his hand in front of his face as though a mosquito had got too close. "Lovely girl. Amazing. But, well, it was never meant to be forever."

That was fair enough. He was still pretty young and looked like a guy who had a lot of wild oats left to sow. Still, I hoped he hadn't broken her heart. She'd gone through a lot for him.

"Ah, good," Alexander said, walking in and surveying the table before he sat down. His blue eyes were opened extra wide, as though he thought that might make him look sober. It made him look like he'd received some very surprising news.

When I got back to the kitchen, I told William they weren't nearly ready for dessert. He didn't look pleased. "I've got this timed to the minute. What about my dessert? It could collapse sitting there waiting for their young lordships to finish the main course."

I held up my hands helplessly. What could I do about it?

Pamela came in at that moment. "What are they doing upstairs?" William asked.

"Everything's fine. Very peaceful. To be honest, they seem more interested in the wine than the food."

Just exactly what William didn't want to hear. Of course, he knew as well as I did that at least two of the men upstairs weren't going to be very interested in his beef Wellington. Not unless it was very, very, very rare.

When the bell rang, I jumped. It actually was just like something I'd seen in very old manor houses in Britain. Only it had been modernized. But still, there was a light that went on that said dining room. I shook my head. Really?

I headed back to the dining room, Pamela at my heels. Why was she following me?

I walked faster and then she walked faster, so we were

practically jogging trying to be the first one in the room. I had no idea what that was even about. Or why I cared.

I managed to get in first, with Pamela so close behind me, her high-heeled shoe caught the back of my Achilles. Ouch.

Alex glanced up. "We need more wine."

I couldn't believe they'd drunk so much wine so quickly. Surely they'd forgotten the bottles still sitting on the side-board. But no—when I looked up, they were gone. They hadn't even bothered decanting the last couple.

I took a couple of the empties, and I thought it would have been nice if Pamela stopped to pick up the half-eaten meals, but she seemed to be asking Jeremy how he'd enjoyed his meal. Winston said, "I need the toilet," and left the room.

I doubted very much that Alex's father was going to open up the cellar for any more precious bottles tonight, but what did I know? He said, "You'll need the key. Ask my father. Or better still, find Briggs. He'll get them for you."

I knew that Briggs was having the night off, but I nodded politely. "And are you ready for dessert? It's really something special." Poor William. I wanted the Gargoyles to at least see his amazing creations. Even though, based on the fact that they'd only eaten about half their dinners, I didn't think they were going to gobble down the dessert.

"Yes, yes. In a minute. After the wine."

"There's also a cheeseboard to come, and port."

"But first bring the wine. And you can clear all this away." He waved his hand over the meals still on the table.

The pair of us cleared away the rest of the food. Charles came in and seemed to struggle to remember where he'd been sitting. He finally located his chair then, before sitting down, studied it. "Alex," he said at last. "I believe there's a wasp's nest in this chair."

"Don't be thick. There are no wasps in April."

He peered closer. "Bees? What about bees?"

"Sit down, you fool."

"Stinging beetles. Nettles, perhaps." He swayed as he finally sat. Oh, I was tempted...

As Pamela and I left with loaded trays, I told her that Alex wanted more wine. "I don't want to go and ask his father for the key to the cellar."

"No. Of course you don't. Don't worry, I can do it."

"But—" She dumped her tray in the prep area, leaving me to take it into the kitchen, and she was gone.

Well, she'd been serving them their dinner up there, so I supposed she was the correct person to ask for more bottles of fancy wine.

Meanwhile, Violet and I finished clearing the plates, and William continued to fret that his desserts would be ruined. "And I've got a lovely Riesling to serve with the dessert. They're boors, those young men, that's what they are. I should have just shoved some fish and chips at them. They'd have been as happy. Probably wouldn't even have noticed."

"But you would have, William," I said soothingly. "You do this for your own sense of accomplishment and pride."

He snorted. "Pearls before swine."

I couldn't argue with him there. We waited for Pamela to return to take the desserts upstairs, but once more she seemed to be missing. "Perhaps she broke one of those ridiculous heels," Violet muttered.

"Lucy, you'd better take the desserts upstairs."

It was my first foray to the other dining room, but I did as

I was told. When I reached the doorway, I could see this four-some was much more sedate but still having a good time. They were laughing at an anecdote from the past. The man with the receding chin was holding forth and was obviously a good storyteller. I waited, knowing that a good server never interrupts the flow of conversation. He ended with, "The don never did find his wig. I believe it's missing to this day. But there was a certain horse at Ascot…" The other three burst into laughter, and the fourth man chuckled along.

I came in with the four desserts and placed them before the men. "Lovely," the storyteller said. "Your caterer's first rate, Hugo. I must take his name. One is always looking for a good caterer."

"He's Rafe's find. And yes, excellent. I must tell my wife about him."

His phone buzzed, and he pulled it from his pocket and glanced at the screen. "And speaking of, that's my wife now. Right on time." He looked around helplessly, and they all told him to take the call.

"Hello, darling. How's London?"

I poured dessert wine and then left the room and went back downstairs to relay the excellent news that, at least among the older crowd, William would probably be getting more business.

"In fact," he said, taking off his apron once again and donning his jacket, "I'm taking the dessert in. Who's with me?"

Violet and I stacked desserts on trays and carried them into the dining room while William came behind us with a special dessert wine.

As we put the desserts down, nobody seemed to even

notice. They were drinking two more bottles of the fancy red wine, so Pamela had got it from the cellar, then, though once again she was off somewhere. I kicked Miles in the ankle and whispered, "Tell William how beautiful the dessert looks."

He looked up at me as though I'd spoken in Japanese. "Pardon?"

"Compliment William on the dessert," I said again. He looked at it and then finally seemed to clue in. "What a beautiful dessert. Did you make this?" he asked William. Miles had been one of the best actors Cardinal College had ever seen. And, even though he was completely wasted, he was able to call on that talent now. "In fact, amazing meal all round." He sounded like he'd never seen anything so beautiful in his life, and I saw William immediately soften under the attention. Taking his lead, a couple of the other guys banged their forks against their glasses, and soon they were all doing it. I supposed that was appreciation.

William said, "Well, as it is St. George's Day, I give you a St. George's Day dessert."

"And I give you a toast," said Alexander, rising.

William poured dessert wine into yet another glass, and Alexander toasted "the fine chef and beautiful serving girls." I was pleased Miles had prodded them into thanking William even though I didn't particularly appreciate being called "a serving girl."

The heir to Bromford Chemists then stood. "And, in honor of St. George's Day, I give you Alexander Percival Brown." He went on a rambling toast that I thought was meant to be thanking Alexander and his family for the use of their home but got lost somewhere along the way.

Alex stood with his phone in his hand. "I'll be a few minutes. Carry on."

Miles said, "Hey. I thought we weren't meant to have phones in here."

"Sorry. It's important."

And then he left. For young men who were supposed to be the height of society and Britain's great hope for the future, they sure didn't have many manners. My parents would have a fit if I had behaved like this during a dinner party.

When we returned to the kitchen, I said to William, "They sure seemed to like your dessert."

"I should think most of them will be sicking it up before morning. They don't handle their drink as well as they think they do."

"Well, they're young yet," I reminded him. Feeling like an old lady at twenty-eight.

"You're right. Their heads will harden as they get older."

"So will their livers."

Nothing remained now but to prepare the cheese boards and pull out the ancient port. We gave them about twenty minutes, and then William sent me in. Once again, Pamela had disappeared. Now that William had brought the dessert wine, they seemed quite happy to suck that back. I thought at this point we could have put rubbing alcohol on the table and they'd have glugged that, too.

We gave them thirty minutes to finish off the desserts before we took in cheese and port. When I got to the dining room again, there was only Randolph Chase still there. I thought he'd have gone with the others, wherever they were, except that he'd fallen asleep. He had his head cradled on his plump hands, and he was snoring softly.

I crept out of the room again, wondering where everyone was, when suddenly I heard someone yell, "Help. Somebody help me."

I didn't know where the noise was coming from, but every cell in my body stood to attention. There was true terror in that tone.

Suddenly I heard more yelling and shouting. "Get the police. Somebody must ring for the police."

Oh, I did not like the sound of those words. What on earth had these foolish undergrads done now? No doubt somebody had skewered themselves with a billiard cue or tripped over their own egos.

Rafe was down the stairs and running toward me before I could even wonder what was going on. "Lucy. Are you all right?"

"Yes. Somebody's yelling, but it sounds like it's coming from downstairs."

He nodded. Glanced in the room where Dolph was just waking up. "Stay here."

And then he opened the door and went running down the stairs.

Randolph Chase woke up. "I say, where is everyone? Was there port?"

"What's downstairs?"

"What? Oh, that's right. They went to play billiards. I said I'd come and join them after my port and cheese."

I left him to it and followed Rafe down the stairs. I didn't know why, but I thought my skills might possibly be needed. There were times when being a witch was a real advantage. I could help people. Not that I was entirely sure I was going to help this bunch of idiots. I'd see what the yelling was about first.

When I got to the bottom of the stairs, I followed the sound of yelling. I found myself in a dark paneled billiard room. Most everyone was there, crowded around the table. But it wasn't a game in progress. It was Pamela. Pamela laid out on the billiard table. I glanced instinctively at Rafe, who nodded in answer to my unasked question.

Pamela was dead.

CHAPTER 6

$\mathcal{I}$ crept closer. Male voices. All talking at once and some shouting, but, as often happens in shock, the sound was just a buzz in my ear. I couldn't keep my eyes off my former friend. Her body was straight down the length of the billiard table with her arms spread out wide. I thought at first someone had posed her to look like a crucifixion, but then I realized the billiard table was covered in red baize, and the way she'd been laid out, especially wearing that white blouse, she looked like the cross of St. George. There was even a belt looped around her legs.

Rafe came over to me and we looked at poor Pamela. He said, "Whoever killed her arranged her body to look like the emblem of the Knights of the Garter."

"Who would do such a thing?" I asked.

I could see now that she'd been strangled. I wasn't a forensics expert, but from the marks on her throat, I had a feeling that belt that was now wrapped around her legs might be the murder weapon.

I hadn't liked Pamela, but I would never want to see anyone finished off like this. She'd only come here tonight to serve food. How could she have made a deadly enemy so quickly?

And why would the killer then pose her corpse to resemble the highest emblem of chivalry?

Behind me came Hugo and his friend, looking slightly winded from pounding down two flights of stairs. Then Violet arrived, followed by William. The last to show was Randolph, looking bemused and half asleep as he came in saying, "What's going on?"

I glanced around. It was a windowless room, lit spot lights inset in the ceiling. The billiards table dominated, but there was also a wet bar tucked in the back and a seating area, presumably for those not playing.

Several of the younger Gargoyles had dispensed with their coats, no doubt getting ready for their game. Winston Bromford cried out, "We only wanted a game of billiards. Oh, I think I'm going to be sick."

"Not in here," Miles said sharply and, grabbing him by the arm, dragged him out.

I pulled myself back together as much as I could. I had some experience of murder, unfortunately, and the first thing I realized was that all these people in here were making a complete mess of the crime scene. I said to Rafe, "We should clear the room. The police won't appreciate all these people in here."

He nodded. Raised his voice. "Hugo? Why don't we all adjourn to the dining room? Leave the scene for the police."

Hugh Percival Brown had taken one look at the body and

turned pale but immediately rallied. "Yes, of course. Come along, everyone. There's nothing we can do for her now." He looked at his son. "Has anyone called the police?"

It seemed no one had, so Hugo said he'd make the call.

He was obviously a man used to making quick decisions and acting on them. Hugo ushered everyone out of the billiards room and told them all to go up to the dining room. Rafe said he'd remain behind to make sure no one else went in. It was too late to keep the crime scene uncontaminated, but at least he could prevent it from getting any more messed up.

Lochlan would have stayed behind, but Rafe told him to go on and quietly asked me to stay with him.

After the group of them had left us downstairs, I said to Rafe, "Why would anyone do that? And why put her body in that bizarre pattern?"

He shook his head. "It's puzzling me, too. Why pose her like the emblem of the Knights of the Garter?"

I didn't want to point the finger of blame at his friend, but I had to point out the obvious. "There is one Knight of the Garter here, you know."

He glanced down at me. "And only three of us, four counting William, are aware of that fact."

"Well, I know I didn't kill her. I know William didn't. And I'm guessing you didn't. But what about Lochlan? Would he have any reason to kill Pamela?"

"And point the finger of blame at himself? Seems unlikely. He didn't even know the girl."

"Are we sure about that?"

Rafe's brows drew together. "Not positive, no. But why

would Lochlan Balfour, who lives in a castle in County Cork in Ireland, know a woman who recently came over from Boston?"

"I don't know, but it's amazing the connections people make with each other. Especially when they've been alive a really long time." I thought about it. "Does he live like a rich recluse, or does he have a job or something?"

"Lochlan Balfour runs a very successful high-tech firm with offices all over the world."

"Including Boston?"

"I see what you're saying. He could have known her, I suppose, but I've known Lochlan Balfour a long time. No one gets to be a Knight of the Garter without great service to the Crown."

"What do the Garter Knights really stand for?"

He paused before speaking. I liked the way that Rafe did that. He wasn't one to throw out an opinion rapidly. He liked to gather his thoughts, so I always knew what he was saying wasn't off the top of his head or random. "The Garter Knights' primary role is protecting and supporting the monarch. They're known for sacrificing themselves for others. They stand for chivalry."

"I understand that, but the world's changed in seven hundred years. I mean, people used to go on crusades and kill all sorts of people back in the middle ages. Maybe Lochlan hasn't moved on."

"You think he killed her as part of a crusade?"

"Maybe she offended his sense of chivalry. Or someone's making a cruel joke about the fact that today is St. George's Day."

"Let me talk to him. In the meantime, don't say anything to the police."

Oh, as if I would. I was so used to hiding things from the Oxford CID, I'd go to jail just for that if they ever discovered all my secrets. Mind you, since my secrets were generally of the supernatural kind, I doubted the Oxford police would believe me anyway.

"If it's not Lochlan Balfour, then who would do that?"

"An excellent question."

I had another one. "What do you think the chances are that somebody came in from outside this house and murdered Pamela?"

He appeared to give my random theory some thought. "I would say it's possible but unlikely."

I nodded. That was my feeling exactly. "That means that the killer is in this house now. It's somebody in the Gargoyle Club."

"Since I would vouch for William, you and Violet, I suspect you're right, Lucy."

There was a commotion upstairs, and then, inevitably, DI Ian Chisholm and DS Barnes came down the stairs and toward us. Hugo was with them, leading the way.

Ian looked at me, and his eyes narrowed slightly. "Lucy. May I ask what you're doing here?"

I motioned to my white blouse and black skirt, not that they really made anything obvious. "I was waitressing."

He looked as though he had trouble believing me. "Moonlighting from the knitting shop? Are knitting sales down? Have people stopped crocheting?"

I really didn't appreciate the sarcasm, especially in front

of Hugo and Rafe. "No. But the caterer's a friend, and I've waitressed for him a few times. It makes me a little extra money, and I enjoy doing it."

He shook his head. "You do get into the most extraordinary situations."

He could say that again.

He looked at my companion, who didn't get off easy either. "And Rafe Crosyer. Are you waitressing too?"

To Rafe's credit, he didn't go all vampire on Ian's ass. "I'm not. I was dining with Hugo."

"And you're all wearing your fancy dress, I see. The Gargoyle Club outfit. Believe me, I recognize it. I thought that club had been banned from Oxford."

"The Gargoyle Club was never an official part of Oxford. It's always been a private gentlemen's club."

"My mistake. Banned from the grounds of Cardinal College then."

Rafe and Hugo exchanged a glance, and their silence pretty much confirmed what Ian already knew.

I heard more footsteps coming down the stairs, and soon we were joined by paramedics.

Hugo unlocked the billiards room door, and Ian and DS Barnes went in with the paramedics right behind them. Soon a forensics team arrived and went in too. The photographer and coroner arrived soon after. I'd been around enough death scenes to know that it would be a busy place for several hours. And that none of us would be allowed to leave until we'd all been interviewed. It was going to be a long night.

Rafe said, "There's nothing we can do here. Come on upstairs."

I didn't want to stand down there near Pamela's remains, so I happily agreed.

"You knew her in Boston, I understand."

"I did."

"Any idea what she was doing here in Oxford?"

"She said she was studying art history. Pamela was very bright but never struck me as the scholar type."

"You don't think a degree from a prestigious university was her goal in coming here?" Was there a sardonic tone? I suspected there was.

"I think she was after her MRS degree. And I think she wanted somebody pretty special."

"Well, any one of these young men tonight would be quite the catch."

I would have laughed if it wasn't such a serious situation. "We sound like a pair of matchmakers plotting in the corridor."

"You'd be surprised. We think matches aren't made anymore. That people have free will in who they marry. It's less true than you think."

We went upstairs, and all the members of the Gargoyle Club were sitting in the dining room in the same seats they'd had before the older men left. Alex went to pour more wine, and his father stopped him. "I think we'd all better sober up. There'll be no more drinking tonight. You all have to give an account of yourselves to the police." He turned to me. "You there. Go into the kitchen and put some coffee on."

I didn't appreciate being called "you there," but coffee was an excellent idea. Dolph still looked half asleep, and the rest of them looked drunk. I nodded and headed back to the kitchen. William was way ahead of me. He already had coffee brewing. "Lucy, I'm so sorry. How are you holding up?" He was such a kind man, and his face was full of concern.

I hadn't really stopped to think about it, but I felt awful. Maybe not having liked Pamela made it even worse to find her murdered. If we'd been friends, I could simply grieve, but I had to accept the fact that a tiny part of me felt relief that she wouldn't be in my life anymore. And what kind of a terrible person did that make me?

"Come and sit down."

"I have to take in the coffee." I was starting to shake all over.

"I'll do it."

I didn't argue. And Violet didn't even wait to be asked. She got up and followed William with the tray of cups and saucers and the cream and sugar.

After they left, I just sat in one of the kitchen chairs and stared out the window into the dark garden. My mind was whirling.

Then a strange woman walked into the kitchen, and I screamed. Just a short, stupid little scream that was more being startled than terrified. Though I was quite terrified.

"Oh, I'm so sorry I frightened you," the pleasant-looking, middle-aged woman said. "I wondered what all the fuss was about. There's an ambulance out front. Is someone hurt?" I glanced up, and I recognized her. But I couldn't think where from. The way she was looking at me, I thought she was going through the same exercise of trying to place me, and then suddenly she said, "Oh, it's Lucy. From the knitting shop. Cardinal Woolsey's."

And when she put herself into the context of the knitting

shop, of course I recognized her as well. "Shannon, how are you?"

Shannon Briggs was a reasonably regular customer in my knitting shop. She'd been knitting a blanket for her aged mother in Scotland last time I saw her. "What are you doing here?"

"I live here."

I was so confused. My head felt like it was filled with cement. "You live here?"

"Well, I live in the flat above the garage. I'm the house-keeper here. My husband is the butler."

"Jack Briggs. Of course."

She said, "I had the night off because the gentlemen were entertaining. But I saw the ambulance. I don't wish to be nosy, but if there's anything I can do to help..."

"There's been a murder," I told her. She'd find out soon enough anyway.

She went pale, and her hand went to her chest. "Someone in the family?"

"No," I hastened to reassure her. "Probably no one you even know. She was here like me, helping serve the food. Her name was Pamela."

"I was so worried something might have happened to Mr. Percival Brown. He works so hard, you know, and he's always traveling and talking to the press. Then he and his wife are at charity functions and I don't know what. I wondered if the stress had caught up with him. I'm so glad he's all right."

"Yes. He's fine. He took charge right away," I told her. "He's very good in a crisis."

Shannon came all the way in and looked as though she

planned to stay for a while. "Pamela. Was she a young woman with long, dark hair?"

I felt my eyes widen. Could this woman have known Pamela? "Yes."

"Heavens."

"Did you know her?"

She went over into the kitchen proper and plugged in the kettle. "No. I'm not even certain it's the same person, but I'm sure the young woman's name was Pamela."

"What young woman? When was she here? What happened?" I'd been certain that Pamela had some sort of an ulterior motive in coming with me. Well, she clearly wasn't the waitressing type. Had she been here before?

Shannon Briggs joined me and said, "She made a fool of me, that's what happened. I was doing the vacuuming one afternoon; it was a couple of months ago. Mrs. Percival Brown was out of town, thank goodness. Hugo was upstairs working in his office, and Alexander was at school, I think. The door-bell rang, and this young woman was standing there. Very attractive and well-spoken, said she was a student friend of Alexander's and they were meeting here to work on a project together. American she was, like you."

Yep, that sounded exactly like Pam.

"She had a bag with the college logo on it and looked exactly like any other student, so of course I let her in. She said that a couple of others would be joining them. I offered to make her tea but she said no, she'd wait until Alexander came home. I left her in the library and didn't think too much about it, and I went about my business. The next thing I knew, there was shouting upstairs. Mr. Percival Brown it was, and he was in a terrible temper. I ran upstairs, all the way to the top floor, where Alex has his own set of rooms."

I wondered how a woman taking her master's in art history could possibly be working on a project with an undergrad.

"I got upstairs, and Hugo turned on me. Told me to throw her out and then he stomped past me. Furious he was. I found her in Alex's bedroom."

"Was she—?"

"Practically naked is what she was. Scrambling into her clothes and looking mortified, I can tell you. She said she'd meant to surprise Alexander. She was his girlfriend, so she said. She'd put herself in his bed, taken all her clothes off, and planned for him to find her there. But, unfortunately, his father saw her first."

"She put herself naked into Alexander Percival Brown's bed?" Man, that woman had been brazen. "In his parents' house? When he wasn't even home?"

"That's right. He lives at the college, of course, but he was expected home for the weekend." The kettle boiled, and Shannon made tea. Even though there was fresh coffee, I wanted tea made by the family housekeeper.

She kept talking as she bustled around getting out cups and milk and sugar. "I'm sure Mr. and Mrs. Percival Brown accept that their son will get up to all sorts of mischief at Oxford. But they're very strict about his behavior in the house. There was a terrible row."

I couldn't even imagine. I felt embarrassed for everybody involved.

"Did you see her anymore after that?"

"Oh, no. There was a terrible row, as I said, and Hugo

called her a common slut and told his son he didn't want her coming around the house again."

I thought that Hugo showed very good judgment. Better than his son.

"Well, she got herself back in the house tonight." And I bet she'd regret it, if she were still alive to regret anything at all.

CHAPTER 7

J wondered why Hugo Percival Brown hadn't thrown Pamela out the second he caught sight of her in his home for a second time. Or had he even remembered? Maybe a woman in serving attire was all but invisible to the billionaire.

Mrs. Briggs said, "Tea will do you good. It's very helpful for shock. Did you bring your knitting?"

I did feel shaken and was only too pleased to remain here in the seating area tucked underneath the window in the kitchen, far away from the Gargoyles. I glanced up as she brought the tea over. "I do have my knitting." Which was weird because I almost never carried it around with me. I only had it because of Violet. I had guessed there might be downtime when we had nothing to do. She'd suggested we bring our knitting along.

Not that there'd been any downtime, between all the courses to be served and the demands for more wine.

Shannon looked pleased. "I find there's nothing like knitting to soothe my nerves. And I have to admit mine are a bit shattered too. I'll pop home and get mine and be right back." She gestured to lighted windows in the carriage house. "That's our flat over there. I won't be a mo."

My knitting was right here in the kitchen inside my backpack. No doubt I'd just make a mess of it, since my thoughts were all in a tangle, but maybe Shannon was right and keeping my hands busy knitting would soothe my jagged feelings. People were always telling me how soothing and relaxing knitting was. I never found that. I usually ended up with a pain between my shoulder blades and something more resembling an abandoned birds' nest than any sort of garment that an actual human being might wear. But I remained hopeful. Running a knitting shop, I was forever being confronted with beautiful patterns and the most luxurious wools, and everybody else seemed to manage to make things. Why couldn't I?

So I pulled out my knitting. I was working on a striped shawl all done in garter stitch. The pattern had promised this was easy, but to me, where knitting was concerned, easy was a synonym for fiendishly difficult. I settled myself in one of the easy chairs. I tried as best I could to ignore the coming and going, all the busyness associated with murder.

When Shannon Briggs came back, she had a cloth bag in one hand and a cigarette butt in the other. She was tsking with annoyance. "It's bad enough they come here and smoke. Did they have to leave their cigarette butts on the lawn?"

I said, "Cigarette butts? How many did Jeremy smoke out there?"

"It wasn't only Jeremy. That dreadful girl was out there smoking with him."

"What dreadful girl?"

She motioned her head toward the downstairs. "The dead girl." I watched her take the cigarette butt and put it in the garbage under the sink. Then she washed her hands quite fastidiously.

"You mean Pamela? She was out there smoking with Jeremy?"

"Yes." She obviously misread my expression, for she said, "I know. Fine waitress she turned out to be."

"No. Shannon, you have to tell the police. Exactly what time did you see Pam and Jeremy sharing a smoke?"

She looked both stunned and horrified. She picked up her knitting and put it down again. "Oh, my goodness. I hadn't thought. Do you think that's important?"

"The police have to establish a timeline. And they'll need to know where everybody was and when. If you can pinpoint both Jeremy and Pamela out in the garden at a certain time, then we know that Pamela would have been killed after that."

"I hadn't thought. Well, I don't really know. I smelled the cigarette smoke. Horrible. I can't bear it. I knew it was one of those boys, and I was going to tell them to go smoke somewhere else. But when I looked out, it was Jeremy, and, well, it looked like he was having a rather intense conversation with that girl."

"Any idea what it was about?"

"I didn't watch them for very long, but I would have said they were having some kind of an argument."

"What exactly did you see?"

I didn't think that Shannon Briggs would ever be a star witness in a trial. She said, "Well, I don't really know. As I said, I smelled smoke, and I looked out the window. And there was Jeremy and he was smoking. That's how I smelt the smoke, of course."

"Right. And was Pamela with him then?"

"Oh, no. I saw her come out of the side door and run across the lawn to join him. She took his cigarette out of his mouth and began to smoke it herself."

Gross. "You mean like a sexy gesture?"

"Perhaps she meant it that way, but he just looked annoyed and dug himself out another cigarette and lit it. Then the two of them stood there smoking, and I heard their voices. Low and, I would have said, angry."

Thanks to William's timer and clock, we had a pretty accurate timeline. I had served that beef at eight thirty-five, and Jeremy was missing. They'd told me he'd gone out for a cigarette. Had Pamela still been there then? Had she overheard it? I thought perhaps she had. So she'd followed him out. Just for a cigarette? Or was there more? I felt like we needed to find out a lot more about Jeremy Pantages. And who better than the housekeeper, who clearly knew Alex's friends.

"Have you known the boys for a long time?"

"Oh, bless you, yes." Now that she was settled with her knitting, I could see that it was helping her talk more easily. I might not love knitting for a whole lot of reasons, but one thing I did notice was women who sat together knitting tended to chat. And while the front of her mind was busy counting stitches and making sure she was following her pattern correctly, another part of her brain was free to make small talk. At least it would seem small to her, but I hoped to glean some very good information from her.

"And how long have you known Jeremy?"

"It must be ten years. Well, the boys went to Eton together. He used to come over sometimes in the school holidays. Although, lately they haven't been so close. Mind you, the boys are all so busy at college. A very clever lot they are. They'll be running this country one day, you know."

Horrifying thought. "Which of them went inside first?"

She glanced up from her knitting. "I beg your pardon?"

"When they were smoking? Which of them went inside the house first? Was it Jeremy or Pamela?"

"Well, I didn't stand there watching them, did I?"

"So you didn't see them go inside."

"No. But I did glance out a little later and...yes, Pamela was going back inside that side door."

"Did Jeremy follow her?"

"No. He stood watching her. He had a funny look on his face."

"Funny look on his face? Like what? Angry? Sad?"

"Confused. I would say he looked confused."

We knitted on for a few more minutes. I suddenly realized that I had done something horribly wrong, and I didn't know what. I made a sound of frustration, not uncommon when I'm knitting. Mrs. Briggs looked up. "What is it, dear?"

"I don't know what I've done." I pushed my knitting toward her, the whole, irritating mess of it.

"Well, I think you've been purling when you should have been knitting." She glanced at the pattern on the table, then up at me. "It's meant to be garter stitch, love. You knit all the rows, no purling. A bit of a beginner mistake." She laughed merrily. "And you running a knitting shop."

Ha ha ha. I tried to laugh at myself, but really, I'd just added one more person in the world who found my knitting a source of amusement.

It took her all of about forty-five seconds to undo what I'd done and get me back to the beginning.

I took my knitting back and thought maybe instead of trying to solve a mystery while two Oxford detectives were on the scene, I might try my hand at my actual job and get better at knitting.

I'd done about six more stitches and managed not to drop one of them, which I was very proud of, when Detective Inspector Ian Chisholm came into the kitchen.

"I'm sorry to interrupt, ladies, but I'd like to speak with all the guests before interviewing you, Lucy. Can you hang on for an hour or so?"

I knew he was being polite when obviously we couldn't leave until they were finished with us. It was already getting late, and we had to open the shop tomorrow. Since Violet was also my shop assistant, it looked like one of us would be opening the shop with not very much sleep under our belts. I suspected that would be me, since I lived right above it. But of course I said, no, that was fine. And then I said, "You'll want to ask Mrs. Briggs a few questions too. She lives in the flat above the garage. She may have been one of the last people to see Pamela alive."

The woman beside me dropped her knitting into her lap. "Really? You think I could have been one of the last people to see that poor girl alive?"

"I think so."

"All right. Mrs. Briggs, if you don't mind waiting too, we're interviewing everyone this evening."

"Oh, that's fine. I couldn't possibly sleep with all this

going on. That poor girl. And the poor family. They so value their privacy. Now, I suppose, this will be all over the news."

I thought it was very likely. Pamela had always wanted to be famous and connected with men of wealth and power. She'd done it, but not in the way she'd planned.

VERY SOON VIOLET and William came back into the kitchen. Violet joined our little knitting circle. William cleaned the already clean kitchen. He polished the sink again. Mrs. Briggs told him it looked perfectly fine and she'd be back in the morning, but he said he needed something to do with his hands.

"William, this isn't your fault," I told him.

"Of course it is. I hired that girl. I didn't even know who she was. I only offered her the job because she said she'd waitressed before and she was a friend of yours."

Oh, great, now I was feeling guilty.

Violet got up and walked over to William. She put a hand on his arm. "Lucy's right, you know. None of this is your fault. There was something odd about that Pamela. If you ask me, she wasn't here to serve food. Did you see those shoes? I've been longing for a pair of those since I saw them in a magazine. They're Louboutin. A thousand quid. And those diamonds in her ears, they were worth a few bob."

"So you're telling me a rich woman who didn't need the money came to work as a waitress."

"Well, maybe she needed the money. Maybe she spent every cent she had on those shoes. I wouldn't blame her; I've contemplated doing that myself. But she looked..." I could see Violet searching for the right word. Finally she came up with, "...well cared for. Her skin had that smoothness that you get from regular facials and the best cosmetics. Her hair was done by a top salon. I don't know, rich women just have a certain look to them."

She turned to me. "Don't they, Lucy?"

I nodded. I knew exactly what she meant.

William seemed to contemplate that. "She did certainly have a different look to her than you and Lucy."

I immediately felt like a poor urchin sitting in the corner. I glanced down at my shoes. They were made for comfort, not style.

"It still doesn't make me feel better. What a dreadful thing."

Violet ushered him over to where we were sitting and forced him to sit down. "I think you need something stronger than tea. What about a glass of that nice port?"

He nodded. "Good idea. It's not like we'll be serving port and cheese after all."

CHAPTER 8

*W*hen Ian called me into the dining room, it was nearly an hour later. He and the sergeant were both there. He was asking the questions, and the sergeant was mainly taking notes. "Thanks for waiting, Lucy."

"Of course."

We'd completely cleaned the kitchen, but the dining room was still as it had been. I supposed even if we'd wanted to clear it, the police would have stopped us.

He got me to sit at the head of the table, where Hugo had begun the evening.

"I'm just going to ask you to tell me everything, being as exact as possible about the timing."

I nodded. I'd expected this. I could see as well as he could that finding this killer depended on being accurate about who'd been where and when.

I said, "Pamela and Violet and I came in the van with William. We arrived about six-fifteen."

"Take me back. I've heard that you were the one who suggested Pamela for the job."

When were people going to stop making that assumption? I shook my head quite violently. "No. It was completely coincidental that she happened to be in my shop when William arrived and offered me the job. She was dropping hints, trying to be invited along, and William, believing that we were close childhood friends, obliged her."

Ian looked at me steadily, but there was a slight twinkle in his eye. "And you weren't childhood friends?"

"Far from it." And then I had to tell him the somewhat embarrassing story of how Pamela had stolen my boyfriend. I emphasized that this was back in high school and ten years ago, hoping he wouldn't guess that the humiliation still smarted a bit.

And just in case he had any ideas, I said, "And by the way, I didn't kill Pamela. It hurt a bit at the time, but he wasn't much of a loss."

"Let's move on then. You arrived at six-fifteen, and then tell me as accurately as you can what happened then."

I took a deep breath. "We were obviously getting the food ready to be taken into the dining room. When I walked in, Rafe Crosyer and Hugo Percival Brown were in the lounge, and they were having a cocktail with two other men I didn't know. One of them was Lochlan Balfour. I never met the fourth."

"Sir Henry Peele."

"By seven-thirty, everyone was in the dining room and we served champagne and appetizers. And by everyone, I mean twelve people. There were the four older members of the Gargoyle Club, and the eight younger members."

Ian nodded. Obviously, he'd already heard this, probably twelve times, but I'd been around him enough to get the idea that a lot of police work was listening to the same story over and over and waiting for that one variation. Or the one person who remembered something no one else had. But in this case, I didn't think I had anything to offer.

"Did there seem to be any animosity in the room?"

It was such an odd question, I was taken aback. I'd been busy trying to think of times and schedules in my head. "Oh. I don't know. I was quite busy. Maybe there was a little coolness between father and son? But no doubt it was extremely humiliating for Alex to be forced to hold his dinner party in his parental home."

Ian's tone was acidic when he said, "Well, the university wasn't going to have it, were they? And no decent restaurant or pub anywhere in Oxford will let those drunken vandals cross the threshold. I'm afraid it was this or nothing."

Right. Nobody would know better than the police what this bunch of posh hooligans got up to.

"And you and Pamela worked closely together?"

I held back my snort, but it wasn't easy. "I didn't really see a lot of Pamela. She was sort of coming and going. Sometimes she seemed to be helping me downstairs because we had eight people, and sometimes she was upstairs. Frankly, she seemed to be doing whatever she felt like."

"Not a very efficient waitress then?"

"She said she had waitressing experience, but I don't think that was true."

He simply nodded, but that disturbing twinkle was back in his eyes. Like he was laughing at me. I decided to ignore it. I talked him through the champagne and appetizer course, through the scallops to the soup. "That's when the older members adjourned upstairs."

"And the eight younger ones stayed here in the dining room?"

"Yes. That was about eight-thirty. They shifted places." I glanced around the table, recalling where everyone was. "So Alex started sitting where I am now. Alex took the place where his father had been. I suppose this is the head of the table." I gestured all the way across to the foot of the table. "Charles Smythe-Richards sat there. Let's see." I made the picture in my mind. Imagined I was Alex. "From Alex's viewpoint, then, to my left was Winston, and to my right was Randolph. Though everybody called the two of them Winnie and Dolph. In the middle was Prince Vikram, and on the other side was Gabriel Parkinson. And then on Charles' right was Miles Thompson. You'll remember Miles; he was one of the actors in *A Midsummer Night's Dream*." Ian had been involved in that production in an official capacity. Since Miles had been a murder suspect at the time, Ian remembered him very well and nodded. "Across the table from him was Jeremy Pantages."

"Did they just sit wherever they wanted? Or was there a seating plan?"

Oh, that was a good question. I tried to remember. "It felt like they were sitting in an order that they'd done a million times. You know the way you do, when you go into a classroom, say, even if the seating isn't assigned, once you've settled in a spot, you tend to keep going back to the same one?"

They both nodded.

"It seemed to me like that was starting to happen, and then Alex said, 'No, Dolph, you sit here. And Winnie, you sit on my other side.' I think that Jeremy was going to sit beside him and stopped and then backed away and sat beside Charles. And then everyone just sort of sat down."

"So, apart from Alex being quite specific about where Winston and Randolph sat, everybody else sat wherever they wanted to."

"That's the way it looked to me."

"Good. Go on."

"We served the beef Wellington then. With the older Gargoyles gone, the younger ones got a lot more relaxed. The wine, by the way, was some fabulous burgundy. According to William, it was a fortune. It came out of Hugo's cellar."

Ian only nodded again. Once more I suspected this was not news to him.

I wanted to make some snarky comment about how much booze they'd been drinking, but it wasn't my place. Ian and the sergeant could do the math as easily as I could. "Jeremy Pantages wasn't there. Alex said he'd gone out for a smoke." I didn't want to steal Mrs. Briggs' thunder, but I said, "Mrs. Briggs saw Jeremy Pantages outside smoking, and with him was Pamela."

"She's sure it was Pamela?"

"Pretty sure. She'd seen Pamela before."

And he could ask Mrs. Briggs for that story, which no doubt she'd be only too happy to tell him. The story of the tramp naked in Alex's bed when Alex wasn't even home.

The sergeant was scribbling notes. Ian said, "So, you served the beef."

"Yes. And they told me to stay out of the room unless they rang the bell." I contemplated telling him about Charles putting his hand up my skirt but decided it wasn't relevant. Besides, I'd dealt with him in my own way.

"And did they ring for you?"

I nodded. "Around nine-thirty, they wanted more wine."

"And Pamela went to get it?" Ian asked me, leaning forward slightly, so I knew this was an important point.

"Yes. Alex told us to ask Hugo for the key to the cellar."

It was hard to remember exactly what had happened and who'd been where, I found, even just in that short period of time. It seemed like there had been so much going on. I put my hand to my head and closed my eyes. "Let me think. I believe that Pamela left then. And I started clearing plates away even though they hadn't finished their dinner, and then that seemed to be the signal for Winston to get up and say he needed to go to the bathroom. I think Jeremy went too."

If I was having trouble keeping all this straight, I couldn't imagine how difficult it was for Ian. But he had heard this story many times by now.

His gaze sharpened on mine. "Did you see Pamela again?"

Had I? I tried to remember. Then shook my head slowly. "She must have come back from the cellar and disappeared again, though, because there were two fresh bottles of the fancy burgundy on the table when I came in to give them dessert."

Ian glanced at his sergeant and then back at me. "In fact, Pamela didn't bring the wine, so Alex sent Miles and Charles to fetch two more bottles."

This was news to me. "They did?"

"So they say. Did you see or hear that?"

"No. As I said, I thought Pam must have come and gone again."

"And everyone was there when you brought in dessert?"

"I think so. Alex had received a text or phone call earlier

and said he had to go outside and take it. I remember because Miles gave him a hard time and said they weren't supposed to have their phones with them during these dinners. But he was back when I served dessert."

"He didn't say who the call was from?"

"He did not."

"Then what happened?"

I put up my hands helplessly. "Half an hour later, I went to check on them, and there was nobody in the room but Randolph. And he was sound asleep on the table."

"Where did the others go?"

"I didn't hear them, but Randolph said they went down to play billiards."

I took a deep breath. This was the hardest part. "I was clearing the table when I heard the yelling."

"And Randolph was the only one in the dining room?"

"Yes."

"And then exactly what did you see and hear?"

"It was absolute chaos, as you can imagine. I ran toward the sound, which was coming from a floor below. Rafe came running down from upstairs and pushed in front of me and told me to stay where I was."

"And knowing you, you didn't stay put," Ian said. He knew me pretty well.

"No. I thought I might be needed. So I followed him downstairs. And when I got there, everyone seemed to be in the billiard room." I had to swallow and take a moment. Seeing someone I had known for such a long time murdered like that wasn't easy to think about, never mind picture again with every detail I could bring up. As though I wasn't going to be doing that every time I woke up in the night. "Pamela was on the billiard table. I think the first thing I remember thinking was how strange that it was a red, felt table. I've always been used to green ones. And then the strange way she was lying. I thought at first she was meant to be imitating the crucifixion." I showed him with my own arms outstretched.

"But then I saw the belt." I felt a coldness creeping up the back of my spine. I wanted to cry and scream and preferably throw myself under the covers of my bed and hug my sweet Nyx. But instead I had to hold it together and try and stay calm. "Well, you saw her. She was laid out to imitate the emblem of the Knights of the Garter."

"Why do you think that was?"

"How would I know? I was just a waitress here."

He only looked at me, and then I said, "It is St. George's Day today. And St. George is the patron saint of the Knights of the Garter."

"You seem to know a lot of history for someone who was just here as a waitress."

"Rafe told me."

"Ah, yes. Rafe. Who, I believe, was also a Gargoyle back in his time here."

"Since he was wearing that fancy dress, I guess so."

"Do you have any idea who would want to kill Pamela?"

"I really don't want to speak ill of the dead, but Pamela had a habit of making enemies. I know it sounds awful to say something so cruel about someone who has recently died and someone I've known so long, but when she stole my boyfriend when we were teenagers? I think she was just practicing. I think that Pamela was a woman who was always looking for the next step in her ladder."

"And you're saying she used men as rungs in that ladder?"

"I think she'd use anyone. Women who were friends, men who were lovers, it was like she was oblivious to the damage she caused. Or she just didn't care."

"Did you get the idea that anyone here tonight had bad feelings toward her?"

"No. I mean, we were all so busy. I mostly noticed how lazy she was. She never seemed to be there when there was food to be taken out or a table to be cleaned. Oh, I did see her talking to Alex, though. In a way that seemed a bit more intense than, "Are you finished with your soup?"

"But you didn't hear what they said?"

I shook my head.

"Thank you very much, Lucy. I can get someone to drive you home."

"That's okay. I'll find a ride." I doubted William would have left without me. And, if I knew Rafe, and I did, he'd be waiting to take me home.

CHAPTER 9

I was right. Rafe was waiting for me. He'd told William to go on ahead with Violet. I wasn't surprised. I was surprised, however, to find that Lochlan Balfour was grabbing a ride back to Oxford with us and that he was staying with Rafe.

"Quite the evening you invited me to," the blond vampire said in his soft Irish accent.

"I can't pretend I didn't suspect there'd be trouble but nothing as bad as this."

"No. I believe you asked me here to prevent drunken rampages and vandalism."

"Anything that would give Gargoyles an even worse reputation, yes."

I didn't say anything, but I was pretty sure murder wouldn't help their reputation.

"According to the housekeeper, Pamela claimed Alex was her boyfriend." I related the story Shannon Briggs had told me about Pam putting herself naked into Alex's bed.

"Yes. His father threw that at his head, too, while we were

sitting in the library being called in one by one to be interviewed by the police."

Lochlan chuckled softly. "I've an idea that Hugo Percival Brown isn't a man who enjoys being ordered about by anyone, especially not the police. He's one as likes to do the ordering."

"Did Hugo suspect Alex of deliberately inviting her so he'd have some female companionship?"

"Or to goad his dad perhaps. I'd wager Mr. Percival Brown expects a great deal from that son of his, including the right marriage."

I didn't like Pamela, but she wasn't completely unworthy. "She was studying at Oxford," I reminded Lochlan. "You have to be very bright to get in."

"Even to study the history of art?" Lochlan sounded scornful. "What happened to true scholarship? Latin and Greek and the classics."

"I'm continually shocked at the subjects people can take degrees in these days," Rafe agreed. "Politics and Policy. Things we used to learn at court."

"And those who failed politics and policy found themselves in the Tower," Lochlan agreed. "Or headless."

Seriously, these two were starting to remind me of my parents and their friends moaning about how much better things were in their day.

"My point is, Pam was bright, and knowing her, she'd have made sure she got a lot of money when she divorced."

"The Percival Browns don't need money," Lochlan said.

I thought about Hugo with his bazillions and his successful companies and his fancy art collection. His title. "What do they need?"

"I don't know, but Hugo's a chess player. I've always thought he runs his business and his life like a game." And his son was a chess piece to be moved around the board? I doubted Alex wanted to be his father's pawn. No doubt he thought he was the king of his own board.

THE NEXT EVENING, we had a meeting of the vampire knitting club. As usual, I headed down from my flat about ten o'clock at night and made sure everything was ready in the back room. The chairs were all set up, and the trapdoor that led down into the tunnels beneath my shop was open. It wasn't that the vampires couldn't come and go even when that door was locked, but they tried to respect that if it was locked, there was probably a reason why I didn't want them coming upstairs.

The first ones to climb up and into my back room were my grandmother, who'd only been a vampire for less than two years, and Sylvia, a glamorous older woman who'd been an actress in the 1920s. She still had an air of celebrity about her and always dressed in the height of elegance. She and my grandmother were best friends and, since my grandmother had been turned into a vampire, had become almost inseparable. They'd had an interesting influence on each other. Since, obviously, they couldn't use mirrors, they had to do each other's makeup. This meant that my grandmother looked far more glamorous than she ever had in life, and that Sylvia was sometimes a bit of a work in progress. Naturally, nobody ever said anything to her. And still with her beautifully cut silver hair, the bone structure, her tall, slim figure and beautiful wardrobe, she always managed to look stunning. My grandmother was wearing a lot fewer of the flat shoes and frumpy skirts and cardigans that she used to wear. Naturally, she'd been able to give up the support hose, and she'd grown more sleek and powerful. She still looked like an older woman but someone you'd look and say, wow, she looks good for her age.

Gran enfolded me in a hug. "Lucy. I'm so glad you're all right. What a dreadful thing. I really don't know what you're doing waitressing anyway. Is the shop doing that badly? You know my investments are doing extremely well, thanks to all the guidance from Sylvia and Rafe and the rest of them. I'd be happy to give you a loan until things picked up."

While I was grateful, I also felt a bit insulted. "I'm doing fine, Gran. The shop's never going to make me a millionaire any more than it did you, but I get by. I don't need to work shifts for William. I do it because it's fun. And I like to support him." I glanced around to make sure Rafe wasn't anywhere near. And dropped my voice just in case, because vampire hearing is about a hundred times better than human hearing, and I didn't want to be overheard. "Besides, I've got my eye out for the next Mrs. William Thresher."

"Yes, poor William. He doesn't get a chance to mingle with mortals very often, does he?"

"No. Not when he's stuck out at Rafe's estate working all the time."

Gran said, "I think Rafe feels it too. Yes, my dear, anything you can do to encourage a romance would be an enormous help."

"And what about this murder? I understand from Rafe

that you knew the victim." This was Sylvia, who wasn't big on wasting time in small talk if there was juicy gossip to be had.

In my experience of vampires, and I'd known this bunch for quite a while now, their biggest problem was boredom. I suppose when your life stretches ahead with no foreseeable end and money isn't an issue and you don't have to hunt for food anymore, boredom would be anyone's biggest issue. Solving crime helped keep their sharp, vampire minds engaged in the same way that knitting kept their nimble fingers engaged, and both helped pass the time.

"I'll tell you everything when everyone's here, then I don't have to keep going through it."

"Very sensible. And how's your knitting coming along?"

That was probably the only question that would make me wish we were talking about murder right now. "Fine," I said in that sort of tight voice that made it clear the opposite was true. Not fine was how my knitting was going.

Both of them knew me well enough to see right through me. "Let's take a look. Where have you gone wrong?"

"Not wrong. Maybe there's something off with the pattern. Did you ever think of that?"

They looked at each other, and it was clear they both suspected that I was at fault more than the pattern.

I let out a huge sigh. "Fine. Do your worst." Actually, I was quite pleased because I'd made a mess of it again, and I knew that between them they would straighten out my knitting in no time. Honestly, it was the only way I could ever finish anything. Every time I got into a tangle, they'd straighten it all out for me and then usually knit a few extra rows to speed me on my way. I had finished a sweater that I was very proud of, for my grandmother. Okay, it wasn't nearly as good as anything she could knit herself, but she wore it quite regularly for sentimental reasons.

Usually, the giving of knitted garments went the other way around. I had a closet and drawers full of the most exquisite dresses, scarves, hats, and lately Sylvia had been making me these cashmere lounging trousers. I now had them in black, red, midnight blue, and a sort of dark gray shot with silver. Until you have worn cashmere lounging pants, well, you just haven't lived. Sylvia presented me with yet another bag. I wondered what color these pants would be. The bag contained a long, black, cashmere sweater in the same wool as my black cashmere lounging pants. Luckily I was wearing them, so I simply slipped off the chunky gray cardigan I was wearing and put the new cardigan over the top. She stepped back and looked rather pleased with herself. "What you need is a nice silk shell and some long beads." She looked me up and down critically. "I have exactly the thing. I'll be right back."

I was thrilled with the sweater. It was exactly my size and both warm and silky to the touch. The gray T-shirt I had on wasn't working, and I wondered what Sylvia would come up with. It wasn't that I needed to dress up for the vampires, but it was kind of fun to play dress-up, especially when I was in Sylvia's jewelry box. That woman had some seriously nice jewelry.

While she was gone, Gran and I had a few minutes to ourselves. We sat down side by side, and she took my hand. I was so used to her cool touch now that it didn't bother me anymore. Instead I sort of found it soothing. "How are things going, my dear?"

"Okay, really. I don't want you to worry about Cardinal Woolsey's. We're really doing quite well."

I didn't want to boast, and maybe it was small-minded of me to feel sort of competitive with my own grandmother, but I liked to keep an eye on how my sales were doing and compare them with how she'd been doing the last few years she'd run the business. At first, after she "died," business had dropped off. Customers had known her for so long, and I was both brand new and didn't know what I was doing or even if I'd stay. But as I'd become more confident and learned more about running a knitting shop, and as her customers had become used to me being in the shop instead of her, business had picked up again. I'd added some innovations. I did a lot more with social media and the website than Gran had ever done and added a few extra classes. I was pretty pleased with how I was doing. I knew that Gran and Sylvia were on the lookout for a franchise opportunity in another city, and that would add to our bottom line. I'd stay put, though. Oxford was my home now.

I turned the question back to her. "How are you?"

She gave me her sweet smile. "I'm adjusting. I think the first year was the most difficult. It's very hard to get used to not being able to say hello when you recognize people. Not even being allowed to go out in the streets of a city you love in the daylight. Being dead but not dead. It's impossible to describe but very peculiar. However, there are advantages. I've got good friends, no aches and pains anymore. My eyesight's better than it was when I was young. I've got so much energy, Lucy. The diet's a little bland, but you get used to it."

"I'm glad." At first I'd been horrified that my poor grandmother had been turned into a vampire. But now that I'd gotten to know them, they were really quite good company. If you wanted a history lesson, you pretty much only had to throw out a question and one of them had been there. I never had to go far to get help with my knitting, and they were very generous with all the garments they made. I think they appreciated that I kept their secrets and didn't mind that their super-secret clubhouse was beneath my shop.

One by one and in twos and threes, the rest of them either came up through the trapdoor into the tunnels that ran under Oxford or, more mundanely, walked in the front door of the shop. By about twenty after ten, all the vampires were settled in their seats, and most of them were already knitting. I shut and locked the front door and pulled down the blinds so that the light didn't appear on the street, and then I walked into the back room. My black cat and familiar, Nyx, came in with me. Nyx was funny about the vampires. She loved some of them, like Rafe, and shied away from others. I wasn't sure if she sensed that they were different or if it was like humans: Some were cat people, and some weren't.

In any case, she liked Gran, and as soon as my grandmother was settled, her needles clacking rapidly away, Nyx jumped up and settled on her lap. It was a lovely, domestic picture. I was so glad that my grandmother was still with me.

The last two to come up from downstairs were Hester, a perennially hormonally challenged teenager, and Carlos, a young Spanish vampire who'd only recently moved to Oxford. I had never seen Hester look so eager. Normally she had a sullen look on her face and such a huge chip on her shoulder, it was amazing she could stand up. I did feel for her, though. It was bad luck getting turned right in the middle of those awful teenage years, but she was a champion whiner. However, she'd recently met Carlos, who was a student at St. Mary's College. I'd seen her develop a practically instant and huge crush on the guy and had worried that it wasn't returned. However, they certainly seemed to be friendly. It was such a pleasure to see Hester with a pleasant look on her face that I really hoped this thing worked out.

From the way we all greeted Carlos, I could tell that everyone felt the same way. He had no idea how grateful we were to him for lifting Hester's mood.

He apologized for his knitting and hoped that we would all indulge him. Then he pulled out the wool and needles that I had sold him only a week ago. I'd advised him to stick to something simple, and so he was working on a scarf. The nice thing about a scarf is it's basically straight edges, and you keep knitting until it's done. Sure, there are lots of fancy ways you can do a scarf with lots of fancy stitches, but sometimes plain old knit one, purl one is the best. By using big needles and big chunky wool, the thing would also grow quite quickly. We'd chosen him a variegated wool in blacks and grays. All the other vampires knit as though they'd been doing it for hundreds of years, which in some cases was actually true. They rarely had to think, and when they got focused, the needles moved so quickly that I actually couldn't focus on them or my eyes would cross. But Carlos was the only other person in the room who was struggling as much as I was. He might even have been worse. Maybe it was small and terrible of me, but his lack of skill filled my heart with glee. Every time he let out a grunt of frustration, a tiny voice inside me said, *yes.*

And every time I let out a similar grunt of frustration, he

glanced up at me and our gazes met. We were together in this at least.

The club was particularly well attended tonight. I suspected it was because of the murder. And I was really happy to have their help and advice. I wanted to talk this through and get their feedback. Pamela had never been my friend, but if she hadn't sought me out, she might still be alive. I couldn't do anything for her now except try and solve the puzzle of who had killed her. And why.

We did our usual show and tell. I always enjoyed seeing what everyone was working on, and often they would take the newest books and magazines that had come into my shop and knit something that I could then display. A sweater that would take some people weeks, and me forever, they'd usually have done overnight.

Alfred displayed a man's vest from the latest Teddy Lamont magazine. Teddy used wools like a modern artist used paints. His creations were bold, outrageously colorful and extremely popular, as was Teddy himself. I heaped on extra praise until Alfred looked down his long nose at me. "This one's for me, but very well, Lucy, I will knit another for you to display in your shop." He said it as though knitting another sweater vest were a huge inconvenience, but I could tell he was thrilled that I wanted to display his work in the store. There was a bit of rivalry over whose knitted work would get the prime display space in Cardinal Woolsey's. I tried to be democratic about it, but honestly, some of the things they turned out were simply more saleable than others.

Mabel, for instance, was a superb craftswoman, but her taste had been formed during WWII, and she couldn't resist re-using scraps of wool and turning out sweaters that might have looked good during the blitz but probably not even then.

Theodore, who had been a police officer in life and now operated a private investigation firm, was busy with cashmere socks. He'd designed them with his monogram knitted into them. He saw me staring, and then I had to ask how it was done. They were so cool. He stopped knitting to say, "Would you like a pair?"

Well, duh.

"And before you ask, yes, I can design you a pattern."

"Are you taking custom orders?" I asked. I could see he hadn't thought of it and told him I thought they'd be very popular as gifts for men. Theodore had an innocent-looking round face like a baby's, which I suspected was one of the reasons he'd been so successful as a police officer in life and was now such a good PI. People tended to tell him things, trusting him with secrets the way they'd trust an innocent baby. His pursed baby lips turned up in a smile. "Yes. Of course. I'd be delighted."

He didn't need the money, and he'd likely donate it to a local children's charity. However, not even a new knitting commission could keep him off the subject of murder for long. "I understand you were present when that poor, young woman was killed. And it was at Hugo Percival Brown's estate, wasn't it?"

I didn't know why he asked that as a question when he knew perfectly well what had happened. Still, I gave him the courtesy of answering. "Yes. I was helping William Thresher. It was a St. George's Day dinner for the Gargoyle Club."

"I've heard the interior's lovely," Sylvia said. "I was in that house once, at a weekend house party with Charlie Chaplin and Ronald Coleman, among others."

"Ah, Ronald Coleman," Mabel sighed. "The man with the velvet voice."

"He was shy in person but quite good fun once one came to know him. The manor house was a lovely place, though rather old-fashioned-looking, as I recall. No doubt the current owner has made some changes." She thought for a moment. "The stables were first-rate. Those who wanted to rode. And as I recall, the cellar was excellent."

I shuddered at the words. It still was excellent as far as I knew.

Theodore interrupted before she took us too far down memory lane. "I understand the murderer is still at large?" Those baby-blue eyes were eager. "Why don't you tell us everything you can, Lucy."

I glanced up and caught Rafe's gaze. He'd been there too but obviously was quite happy for me to tell the story as I knew it. So I did. As I had told the police, I went through everything I remembered from the time I got there until the time I left.

Even as they knitted with incredible speed, I knew that every one of them was listening intently. Even Silence Buggins, the notoriously chatty Victorian, managed to keep her mouth shut while I got through the whole story.

She was, however, the first one to have an opinion when I'd finished. "Obviously, it was Lochlan Balfour who murdered that girl."

It was such an odd thing to say that eighteen vampires stopped knitting and stared at her. And one human did the same.

CHAPTER 10

*I*t was Rafe who answered her. "Lochlan Balfour? Why on earth would he kill a girl he didn't even know?"

Silence was wearing a high-necked cotton blouse with a cameo brooch at her throat. A spray of flowers was pinned to the lapel of her jacket. I recognized them as human hair flowers. It was a new hobby that she'd recently taken up. Her long, brown skirt hung to the ground, and her boots were touching at the ankles, as no doubt her knees were touching. Her hair was done in the same updo she'd been wearing probably since she was fifteen years old, about a hundred and fifty years ago. So when Silence looked prim, she didn't have to work at it very hard. "It's the only thing that makes sense. Lucy described that girl as being laid out like the emblem of the Knights of the Garter. They're a chivalric order. And Lochlan Balfour was a Knight of the Garter in life. Therefore, it must have been him."

"But why?" Rafe pressed.

"To protect someone," she said as though it were blindingly obvious.

I said, "But isn't chivalry about protecting women?"

Dr. Christopher Weaver, who'd been as stunned as anyone else, picked up his knitting again. "I wonder if you could be right, Silence."

Now it was Silence's turn to be surprised. Those weren't words that were said to her very often. "Well thank you, Dr. Weaver. It's nice to know that someone listens to what I have to say. Of course, back when Mr. Tennyson was alive—"

Christopher Weaver interrupted her without ceremony. "Yes, but to answer Lucy's question, chivalry is an order. It's only in recent years that the term has been more about men being polite to women. Originally it was about fighting for all that was right."

The others were listening, and all had resumed their knitting. Except for Rafe. "Lochlan Balfour isn't a murderer. He's currently a guest in my home. The only reason he's not here with me tonight is that he doesn't care for knitting. I'm not in the habit of harboring murderers under my roof."

"Not knowingly," Silence said.

"All right," Dr. Weaver said quickly to keep the peace. "It was just a theory."

I wondered why Rafe was quite so certain his friend had nothing to do with it.

There was a slightly awkward silence, and then Sylvia broke it. "Tell us more about the victim, Lucy. I understand you knew her."

And how I wished I hadn't. As briefly as I could, I once more told the story about Pamela. Of how she'd stolen my boyfriend in high school. A humiliation that I really didn't like having to relive again and again. "And then we lost touch." I vividly recalled the moment that she had burst back into my life again. "Until a few days ago." I told them how she'd come in just before William, and how he'd ended up inviting her to be a server along with me.

"Are you sure that was a coincidence?" Sylvia asked me.

"How could it not be?"

She shook her head. "I don't know. I don't know at all. But clearly, she was known there. She'd claimed to the house-keeper that she was Alex Percival Brown's girlfriend."

"Yes. Which he flatly denied," Rafe said. He'd been with the other Gargoyles, old and young, while the police were interviewing everyone, so he'd heard Alex loudly insist she wasn't his girlfriend and hadn't known she'd be there."

"Do you believe him?"

"I don't know," Rafe said.

I told them that Shannon Briggs had seen Pamela smoking with Jeremy Pantages and she'd believed they were arguing.

Theodore raised his eyes from his knitting. "I wonder if she had intended to go to that dinner all along."

I'd been wondering that too. "But how could she have known about the dinner? It was kept secret, and she couldn't have known William would be catering. She came into Cardinal Woolsey's before William got there. It really looked like a coincidence."

Sylvia said, "Every good actress knows that timing is everything. One enters the scene at the precise moment so that the tension rises." She looked at all of us. "I'm always wary of coincidence."

Rafe looked at me. "Didn't Pamela say she wanted to invite you to a party for her art history professor?"

I nodded. "But I think she made it up. I'm positive she only came to my shop to try and wangle an invitation to the dinner party at the Percival Browns'. But I still don't understand how she pulled it off."

Rafe turned to Theodore. "Can you find out who her art history tutor was? I think it would be worth finding out whether the don in question actually does have a book release coming out."

I could see he was following a train of thought of his own. I gave him a moment and then said, "Why?"

Now he turned his attention to me. "There had to be a reason why Pamela wanted to get inside that house. We already know it wasn't the first time she had attempted it. According to her, she was there because she was Alexander's girlfriend. But he denies that."

I thought there were a whole lot of reasons why Alex might deny having been intimate with Pamela. But I hadn't really considered the possibility that he was telling the truth.

Theodore answered, "You think she was using Alexander to get into the house?"

Sylvia spoke up now. "Oh, I think I see where you're going with this."

I was glad she could, because I had no idea.

Sylvia nodded. "The art collection owned by Hugo Percival Brown is famous. He and his wife are both collectors. Genevieve Percival Brown is said to have quite the eye."

Rafe answered dryly, "And quite the budget."

I wondered if she'd outbid him on something. I bet she had. But whatever her budget was, I suspected that Rafe's pockets were deeper. If he stopped bidding, it was probably on principle.

I finally saw what he was getting to. "You think that she was planning to steal one of the priceless paintings?" She'd certainly spent enough time while we were there with her nose practically touching the artwork in the dining room. She'd definitely shown more interest in the art than she had in serving dinner.

Theodore said, "It's an interesting possibility and certainly a trail worth following. I'll find out more about this don she was allegedly hosting a party for."

"Hang on," I said. "Are you suggesting that an Oxford don could be somehow involved in art theft?"

"An open mind, that's all I'm suggesting."

Gran said, "I read about an art theft quite recently at one of the Oxford colleges. Three Masters were taken, I believe. One was a van Dyck."

Rafe nodded. "That's right. And there were some significant drawings by da Vinci."

"But didn't they get those back?" I was impressed that Gran kept up so well with current events, seeing that she herself wasn't current anymore.

Rafe nodded. "The reality is that art heists of very famous paintings rarely turn out well."

I could see his point. "I guess you can hardly steal van Gogh's *Sunflowers* and then try and sell it on eBay."

"I wouldn't put it so crudely, but essentially you're correct. Statistically about half of the great artworks that are stolen are eventually returned." Half wasn't the greatest odds.

"What about the other half?"

"Ah. Two possibilities. There are collectors. Very, very

wealthy and secretive collectors who yearn for certain artworks for their collections. These people will pay an enormous amount of money for a painting they truly desire. But the reason is usually more prosaic. People steal paintings the way they'll kidnap a family member."

I was completely confused. "For ransom?"

"Essentially, yes. The insurance companies will usually pay a great deal to have a painting returned. It's still cheaper than paying out on the claim."

"Are you thinking that Pamela was somehow involved in something like that? That she was going to steal one of the Percival Browns' Great Masters?"

It didn't really sound like Pamela. Although the Pamela I knew would stop at nothing if it was of benefit to her. I wasn't completely buying it, though. Theodore, however, was quite intrigued by the notion. As much as anything, I thought, he liked the idea of poking around in the world of secret art dealings. "I'll get right on it. And report back at our next meeting."

It was nice to have the extra help. As Rafe said, every lead was worth following.

Sylvia continued, "What happened after high school was finished? What happened to Pamela after that?"

"I don't know, and I don't care."

"I think it would be well worth your while to find out a little bit more about your former friend. I could tell you stories of film stars and the kinds of people, both male and female, who would go to any lengths to have them. Your Pamela almost sounds like one of those. Always reaching for the stars."

I thought back to my high school days. "Well, Sam wasn't

much of a star, but—"

"No. But you had him, so she wanted him. People like that are always reaching for the unattainable. The leopard doesn't change its spots, Lucy. If that young woman was acting like that when she was a teenager, I'd be very interested in her career over the last ten years."

"Do you think it would have anything to do with what happened to her? You think someone was getting revenge because she stole their man?"

"I don't know. But I think it would be worth finding out."

I agreed. And told them that I would do some digging. I hadn't remained friendly with Pamela, but I was pretty sure that somewhere in my friends' group, I could find someone who knew exactly what she'd been up to in the last ten years.

"Okay," I said, "I'll look into Pamela's background in the last ten years, but I don't have time to look into everyone who was at that dinner." Not that I'd have any idea how to do it anyway. I was pretty sure some of the knitting club would have both the time and some ideas about the other people that had been at that dinner. I was not disappointed.

Theodore said, "Who of the eight young men at that dinner had the opportunity? Let's start there and then eliminate our suspects and focus on the ones who could have done it. Then we can work on motive."

I went through my timeline one more time. At the end of my recital, it was pretty clear that any of them could have killed Pamela. Between going out for smokes and the bathroom and down to the cellar to get wine, and I didn't know what else, everybody had ended up disappearing at one point or another throughout the dinner.

"Right," Theodore said. "We'll have to share the suspects between us. I'll take Randolph Chase."

"Why him?" As the only professional investigator among us, I would have expected Theodore to choose someone who was most likely to be guilty.

"Because I investigated his grandfather." He said it with such satisfaction that I had to know more. He obliged. "It was before social media, when everyone knew everyone else's business. There were rumors he was profiteering off the war." He shook his head. "Very bad form. Very bad."

"And? Had he?"

Theodore shook his head, looking annoyed. "I could never prove it. But I think he was guilty."

Sylvia spoke up next. "Well, I try not to be a woman who kisses and tells, but I was rather friendly with Vikram's...good heavens, it must be his great-grandfather. The Maharaja of Pune." She looked rather coy. "The rubies that man gave me. One of the nicest gifts I've ever received from a gentleman." The way she said it, I suspected there were quite a number of other very nice gifts. Sylvia had enjoyed her time in the spotlight. And out of it.

"And he gave me my Matisse." She said it the same way she'd have said he gave her a pair of bedroom slippers.

No one else looked surprised, but I think I squealed. "He gave you a Matisse?"

"Oh, yes. It hangs in my flat in Paris. I'll take you there sometime."

"He gave you a Matisse."

She smiled with great smugness. "Gertrude Stein was terribly annoyed. She'd had her eye on it herself. One of his first paintings of the dancing women. It's lovely. Of course, in those days, you could pick up a Matisse or a Picasso for a song. Now they're very collectible."

Very collectible wasn't how I'd have put works that hung in the great art galleries of the world. But I was getting sidetracked. "Okay. You're on Vikram." I looked around. "Who else?"

Hester said, "Well, obviously, Carlos should investigate Gabriel Parkinson."

We all looked at her. "He's half Colombian." She said it as though she was saying "duh."

Carlos looked quite surprised. He turned to her. "Hester, I'm Spanish. This young man is from South America."

She rolled her eyes. "I know that. I know where Colombia is." Which suggested to me that she probably didn't. "But you both speak Spanish, don't you?"

Okay, she had a point there. "Fine. I will see what I can find out about this Gabriel Parkinson. And you will help me." Which of course was exactly what Hester had wanted, so her irritation turned to satisfaction.

Dr. Weaver said that he would look into Charles's background.

Theodore looked at the list. "What about this Miles Thompson?"

I said, "I'll take care of Miles. I know him. We were together in the production for *A Midsummer Night's Dream.* Theodore, you remember. You were a set painter for that production."

"Good Lord. Was he the young fellow who played Lysander?"

"That's right."

"We had him down as the murderer at one point."

"Yes. But he didn't do it. He was innocent."

"Are you sure you're up for this, Lucy? Perhaps you're a little too close to him. Are you certain that you could be impartial?"

"I wouldn't shield him for murder, if that's what you mean. Miles is a nice guy, but let's face it, he's a player. He was supposedly in love with Sophia Bazzano. Now she's history."

Theodore looked quite disappointed. "Do you mean to tell me, after all that poor, young woman went through, they split up?"

His lack of loyalty to Sophia didn't look very good on Miles.

"What an utter cad," Theodore said. That was half the fun of hanging around with a bunch of vampires. They said things like, "What an utter cad."

But as charming as the sentiment was, it was sort of true. Still, Miles was my friend. "Maybe Sophia broke up with him."

"We can only hope."

Having finally agreed that I could be the one to talk to Miles, Theodore said, "That only leaves Alexander Percival Brown."

Rafe said, "I've known his father for years. I've known the family ever since he was born. I can look into him."

Theodore gave him the same look he'd given me. "You're hardly an impartial observer."

Rafe stood up and stared down at Theodore sitting suddenly uncomfortably on his chair, knitting needles abandoned. "If Alexander had anything to do with the young woman's murder, believe me, I will inform you of it."

"Fine," Theodore said, looking somewhat nervous.

Once again, Sylvia broke the awkward silence. "Excellent. I only wish there were more that we could do. Still, I shall enjoy finding out more about the maharaja's family. Lucy, what's the great-grandson like?"

"Gorgeous. Excellent manners. Really, really charming."

She nodded, looking pleased. "Very much like his great-grandfather then. You know, Lucy, you could do a great deal worse than to—"

Rafe interrupted, looking thunderous. "Lucy will not be chasing after some overbred Oxonian who could be a murderer. Is that clear?"

CHAPTER 11

*H*e might have been looking at Sylvia, but I suspected his words were intended for me.

I was half tempted to take offense at his controlling manner, except that I knew how much Rafe cared for me. Besides, I wasn't interested in Vikram. But a girl could look, couldn't she?

There were a couple of people I knew who might have stayed in touch with Pamela. I chose to start with Sarah Levinson, as she had been one of the key organizers of our tenth anniversary high school reunion. I hadn't been able to attend, obviously, since I was living in England, but I was pretty sure that Sarah kept up with everybody. I sent her a quick email, and she got back to me flatteringly quickly. I said it had been such a long time since I had caught up with anybody from back home that I wondered if she had some time to Skype. She sounded delighted to hear from me, and we set a time the following day for my evening and her afternoon.

If anyone would know what Pamela had been up to in the

ten years since we had left school, Sarah would. Or if not knowing herself, she'd know someone who did.

Of course, since I hadn't attended my tenth year high school reunion, and I knew what a gossip Sarah was, I dressed myself and did my makeup and hair for my Skype catchup chat, putting almost as much effort as I would have had I actually gone to the ten-year reunion. No doubt she'd be telling everyone we knew that she'd caught up with me, and I didn't want her telling them how badly I'd aged.

When we connected, I felt suddenly transported back to high school, to metal lockers that banged and gossiping in the girls' bathroom. Sarah looked genuinely thrilled to see my face. Like me, she'd gone to a lot of trouble with her appearance. At the same time, we said, "You look great!"

She was a little rounder in the face, and her hair was a more stylish version of the long, straight curtain she'd worn a decade earlier, but she was otherwise the same. It was like falling back in time. "Lucy. It's been so long. Where have you been? What are you up to? Tell me everything. How are you? I heard you had a kind of breakdown after Todd. You went all the way to England!"

Seriously? That was the word? Oh, I was glad I was talking to the biggest gossip my high school had ever seen. I straightened her right out. "Todd was an ass, and I am so much better off without him." All true.

I told her I loved my life in Oxford. Also true.

"And are you seeing anyone?" she asked in that soft, pitying tone people use when they suspect you'll die alone surrounded by a couple of dozen cats.

I could tell her I was being wooed by the most incredible man, perfect in every way but one. Instead, I said I was so busy with my shop and busy social life that I didn't want to settle down. Then I politely asked about her.

Twenty minutes later, she was still talking. Her husband was the sweetest, funniest, best-looking man in the world. Their two-year-old was a child prodigy and so beautiful that people stopped her in the street to compliment her, and she was expecting a second child. They'd bought their dream house in a small town where it was more affordable, and there were wonderful schools for her children, who were definitely going to need gifted programs. Yes, even the one still in utero.

I was genuinely pleased for her, for even though she was a real gossip, she was nice. So nice I almost wondered if she was still in contact with Pamela, but sure enough, after I listened to catchup stories on a few of our other classmates, I brought up Pamela.

There was a slight pause. "She didn't make it to the high school reunion either."

This was a blow but not surprising. Unless someone in our class had turned out to be a billionaire, I couldn't imagine that Pamela would waste her time. "Do you know what she's up to? I thought I caught a glimpse of her the other day in Oxford."

"Yes. I talked to her after she got divorced. I was so surprised. Hadn't talked to her in ages. I think she wanted to make sure I heard her side of the divorce story."

"Right." So the correct gossip would get spread.

"She said she'd been accepted to Oxford. I told her you were in Oxford and that she should contact you."

That got my attention. "So she knew I was here?"

"Yes. I told her you were running that knitting shop. And she said she'd make sure and drop by."

"So what's she been up to for the last ten years?"

"Well, didn't you hear? She married Conrad Forbes. He was on one of those 'richest under forty' lists. Pam turned into a real socialite."

"No. I hadn't heard that." Until Pamela made sure to tell me herself. I'd gone out of my way not to hear anything about Pamela. "What happened?"

"She ran an art gallery in Boston." Sarah's face got that eager look I remembered when she had something juicy to share. Even though we were on video chat, she still leaned closer to the screen so I could see a line where she hadn't quite blended her eye shadow. She dropped her voice as though we might be overheard. "Okay, this is kind of snarky, but I heard that she cheated on him and then got a really good divorce lawyer and *she* went after *him.*"

That sounded like classic Pamela, to hurt a man badly and still go after his money. "So she got a good settlement?"

"Huge. The woman has no shame. She cheated on him, broke his heart and still grabbed the victim role."

In fact, Pamela had recently grabbed the biggest victim role of her short life, but I didn't want to stop the flow of gossip by telling Sarah our old friend was dead.

I thought again about why someone with all that money would want to be a waitress on a one-night gig.

"She made out like a bandit."

"Why did she move to the UK?"

"She got a lot of money, but his friends turned on her. I'm not sure her gallery could have made it without him funding it. Or maybe she just got bored. Who knows? Next thing, she was headed for Oxford."

"Doesn't it seem strange to go back to school after she'd been running her own business?"

"If you ask me, she wanted a title."

"What?" I was startled, but as her words sank in, I saw the sense in them.

"Well, she watched a certain American TV star nab herself a prince, and I think Pamela decided she wanted one too."

I shook my head in disbelief. "There aren't so many princes. And most of them are already married."

"Obviously not a prince but, I don't know, a duke or an earl or something. She had all the money she'd ever want, and she was still young and beautiful, and she was always smart. Why not grab herself a title?"

This felt like something out of another era. Like a Vanderbilt setting sail in the Gilded Age to fund a destitute British aristocrat with American cash in return for a title. Did people do that anymore?

"Remember Kate met William at university. Most people meet their mates at school or at work." She flipped her hair back over her shoulder. "My grandpa always used to say, 'If you want to get rich, rob a bank. That's where the money is.'"

As homespun wisdom went, I'd heard better. Still, it was an interesting theory. "Did she have any luck?"

"We weren't that close. I follow her on Instagram."

We chatted a little more about former friends, and she said, "Do you still keep in touch with Todd?"

I tried to sound airy as I told her that I didn't. I didn't want to know what Todd the Toad was up to, but Sarah wasn't the kind of person who picked up on subtle nuances, and she happily proceeded to tell me that Todd was back with Monica and she'd heard they were planning to get engaged.

I didn't wish the pair harm, but it did irk me that he was thinking of marrying the woman he'd cheated on me with. But then, maybe all that meant was that they were truly meant for each other. And that evolved, zen-master thought lasted about a second before I decided that all it meant was that two slimy cheaters deserved each other.

After we'd said goodbye and "let's do this again soon," I went to Pamela's Instagram account. I hated doing it. I wouldn't have wanted to keep up with her curated version of herself in life, and it was even worse in death. I scrolled and looked and read the short captions. Pam's Instagram was like the "here's what the young and beautiful are doing" section of a high-end glossy magazine. She looked stunning in every photo, of course, and she was always pictured with people as polished and connected as she wanted to be. Here she was at Henley Regatta and on Ladies Day at Ascot in one of those hats that looked like a flying saucer had landed on her head.

I didn't recognize the women, though they looked like the female versions of the Gargoyles, polished and posh, but escorting her at Henley was a man I did recognize. Jeremy Pantages. Interesting. According to the date, she'd been at Henley last July on the arm of Jeremy. Before she'd even started at Oxford. What did it mean?

Had she really come to Oxford, not for a degree, but to bag a title? No doubt, she wouldn't be the first.

I messaged Miles to see if he wanted to get together for a drink. I figured I was all dressed up and had my makeup on and I might as well do an extra bit of sleuthing. He texted back that I should come up and meet him at the college. Miles said he was busy studying and needed another half an hour, but then he'd be happy to meet me at the pub. Since Cardinal College was just up the road from me on Harrington Street, we agreed to meet at The Bishop's Mitre.

With half an hour to kill, and still mulling over what I'd learned from Sarah, I called Rafe's butler and independent caterer, William. When he heard my voice, he said, "Lucy. How are you holding up? I feel so terrible that I dragged you into this ghastly mess."

"It wasn't your fault, William. But I have a question for you. I've been thinking about how much of a coincidence it was that Pamela would turn up at my shop right when you were coming to offer me a catering job. Did the Percival Browns know who you were using for staff?" It was a bit of a long shot, but I couldn't think why she would have managed to be in my shop right when William arrived. I knew coincidences happened, but this was a pretty big stretch to be a genuine coincidence.

"Yes. I talked to both Alex and his father. They wanted to go over the menu with me, and his father made it clear that in the past there's been some trouble with women. He asked who I was planning to hire as wait staff, and I told him about you."

"How did you describe me?"

"I told him exactly who you are. That you are a little older than the other boys, a very down-to-earth person who runs a knitting shop, and how wholesome you are."

Not exactly the most flattering description. "Wholesome?" I sounded like an apple-cheeked country girl who woke up at five in the morning and milked the cows.

"Well, I may have downplayed your attractiveness, but I also knew that Hugo Percival Brown and his son had nothing to worry about with you."

Okay, that made me feel slightly better. "Did you tell them that you were going to ask Violet?"

"Probably. I no doubt described her as your knitting shop assistant."

There really was something about a knitting shop that immediately conjured a woman who was probably older and perhaps more dowdy than either Violet or I liked to see ourselves. "Did you tell them that you would be looking for a third waitress?"

"I don't remember. I may have. It's the sort of thing I do, think aloud. Or they may have asked how many staff were coming. I can't remember."

"Okay. I'm really sorry that gig turned out so badly for you."

"Me too. But I hope it won't put you off helping me out again?"

"Anytime, William. All you have to do is feed me and I'm there."

I walked into The Bishop's Mitre and immediately spotted Miles. He was tucked away in a corner, and he had a beer and a novel in front of him. I caught sight of him before he saw me, and I thought if they used that picture in advertising for Cardinal College, women from all over the world would be flocking here. He had that kind of sexy, shabby, intellectual look about him that was irresistible. I could see I wasn't the only woman who'd noticed him. Probably because he was reading, nobody was bothering him, but I thought the second he put that book down, he might have some company. As though he felt my gaze on him, he glanced up, and his face broke out into a smile. He stood up and came toward me and gave me a hug, thereby earning me a few new enemies in the single, young women department. "Lucy, it's so good to see you. What can I get you?"

I looked at his beer and said I'd have the same. I settled myself in the seat across from him, and while he was getting me the beer, I picked up the novel. I should have known better. It wasn't a novel. It was Homer's *Iliad*.

When he returned, he said, "Thank you for saving me from Greek classics."

"Is it any good?"

He glanced at me quizzically. "Compared to what?"

Right. My usual go-to authors were in no danger of being supplanted by this new writer I'd stumbled onto.

I sipped my beer and wished quite desperately that I was here hanging out in a student pub with a great-looking guy with nothing between us but a battered Penguin paperback. But I wasn't. "I can't stop thinking about the other night and poor Pam getting killed."

His expressive eyes grew sad. "It was awful. I can't stop thinking about it either."

"If we all just try and figure out exactly where we were and when, then I feel like we might be able to pinpoint who did this thing."

He didn't look very surprised that I was poking my nose into detective business, but then he'd seen me at work before. "It couldn't have been anyone in that house, Lucy. I've been thinking about it. Somebody must have come in from outside. It's the only thing that makes sense."

I thought the way she'd been laid out like the emblem of the Knights of the Garter made that very unlikely, but for now I didn't argue with him.

"I heard that you and Charles went to the wine cellar to get more wine."

He nodded, and I could tell he'd been thinking of little else, as we all had, since the dinner. "That's right. Alex told me and Charles to go and see about the wine, because Pamela hadn't come back with it. He gave us a map so we could find it."

The wine cellar was big enough it needed a map?

"Did you go into the billiards room by any chance? On your way there?"

He nodded. "We had an idea that we might play later. It was Charles who suggested the game after dinner."

"And there was no one in there?"

"Pamela wasn't lying on the table dead, if that's what you mean."

That was exactly what I had meant. "Okay. Sorry I interrupted."

"So we went along to the cellar and fetched the wine."

"Wait, back to the billiard room. Was there anything at all out of order? Anything you noticed?"

He cocked his head to one side. "Lucy, you saw how much we'd all been drinking."

"Lights on? Lights off?"

He squinted, and I felt like he was in pain, dragging at his drink-fuddled memories. "On. They must have been because

I remember looking at the wet bar in the corner and thinking you could always find a drink in that house."

"Good. Now tell me about the wine cellar."

He looked at me like I was not the brightest. "It's a cellar. It has wine in it."

"Okay, I did a tour one time in France, and these wine cellars go on for miles and there are corridors and corridors of them with boxes stacked up to the ceiling and you could get lost if you didn't have a map. Is it like that?"

"Well, it's not as grand as that, but it is a bit of a warren. The wine collection at that estate is at least a hundred years old. It's dark and cool and is packed with dusty bottles."

"And nothing seemed out of the ordinary?"

"Not that I noticed." He sipped from his beer. "But in the state I was in, if I'd have seen an elephant, I'd have wished him a good evening."

"But if you'd seen Pamela, dead or alive, you'd have remembered that?"

"Of course."

"And then the two of you went straight back upstairs to the dining room."

He started to say yes and then stopped himself. "No. Charles needed some air."

"He needed some air?" What was he, a Victorian lady whose corset was too tight?

Miles looked a little embarrassed. He stared down at his beer and said, "There's no toilet downstairs on that level."

Gross. "So when you said he needed air, you mean he was going outside to pee on the bushes?"

"I didn't hang around, but I suspect so."

"So he went outside the downstairs door."

"Yes."

Well, that was interesting. Or was it? Had he just gone outside, relieved himself and come back in that same door? Had he wandered around outside? From the amount of alcohol those guys had been consuming, I could quite imagine that he might have walked around the garden to try and get his wits back together. Maybe come in the front door even.

"I was in and out, obviously, during the evening, but was there any kind of argument, or did anyone talk about Pamela?"

"Not really, because she was there, but it was definitely like putting the cat among the pigeons."

"She caused trouble?" And no surprise there. "Did she know them before?"

"Yeah. I was surprised to see her there. I've seen her with Alex a few times." He fingered the Homer, flicking his thumb up and down the pages. I waited. "She made out like it was a great joke. Like she was posing as a waitress when she was really one of us, but something about it felt off. Jeremy looked murderous." He suddenly glanced up, and those expressive eyes widened. "Figuratively speaking."

I wondered.

"Because Alex and Pamela were an item?"

"I don't know what they were. Alex isn't one to tell you all his business. And he's not looking to settle down, if you know what I mean."

Miles could have been describing himself. "You mean he likes to play the field."

Miles leaned in and dropped his voice. "There are a lot of really great girls in Oxford. Why would he limit himself?"

And I knew then that he'd been just as aware of all those young women gazing at him adoringly while he read his classics as I had been.

"Did Pamela know she was one of many?"

"Like I said, I don't know what their relationship was. They may have just been friends."

"What about Jeremy?"

He went back to running his thumb up and down the closed pages of his book. "They aren't my closest friends. Alex, Jeremy and Dolph all went to Eton together. They go way back, but I've only known them a year or so. I thought Pamela had been seeing Jeremy. In fact, it might have been Jeremy who introduced her to Alex. I don't know. But something was up between those two that night. There was definitely tension. Normally Jeremy always sat beside Alex at those dinners, but he was at the other end of the table."

I thought of that Instagram photo featuring Jeremy and Pamela from last July. Had Jeremy been a stepping-stone to Alex? The one she really wanted?

"How long was it until Charles came back into the dining room?" I asked Miles.

He looked at me with a pained expression on his face. "That was pretty late into the evening, Lucy. I'm sorry to say it's all a bit fuzzy."

I was trying to think of more questions to ask him. Particularly I wanted to know what they'd been talking about when I hadn't been in the room. But I doubted that Miles would be too quick to share the kinds of things that eight drunk undergrads would talk about when I wasn't in their presence. I was still mulling over how to tactfully begin when he raised his hand in a wave and I turned around to see the Colombian, Gabriel Parkinson, coming in. With him was a stunningly beautiful young woman, and I nearly choked on my beer when I saw that behind them was Carlos and, looking far more cheerful than the last time I'd seen her, Hester. She looked less than pleased when she realized that I was at the table they were about to join, but by that time, we were pulling in stools from other tables and turning our group of two into a group of six.

Miles made everybody welcome and said, "Do you all know each other?"

He then saved me from having to lie by automatically going around and introducing us all.

Gabriel said, "I was practicing my Spanish with Carlos. It's amazing how quickly it gets rusty. I miss hearing my own language."

I could imagine. Sometimes I missed hearing my own accent. Once in a while it would be nice to hear the word chips and not have to translate in my own head to french fries. Or be able to say trash can and not have to substitute the word bin. Anyway, it was nice to see that Carlos and Gabriel had found a common pastime.

Hester sat maybe a little bit closer than was entirely necessary to Carlos, but he didn't seem to mind. Gabriel's friend?—date?—was blonde and so skinny she must either be an anorexic or a model or both. She was awfully pretty, though. Naturally, Gabriel and Miles had the murder in common and immediately asked each other if they'd heard anything. Both shook their heads. I thought they looked worried and wondered what Miles hadn't told me.

I glanced around, hoping that the rest of the guys from

the dinner party might show up, but no such luck. I asked, "How is Alex doing?"

I knew I'd pushed the right button when Gabriel and Miles exchanged another glance and their expressions grew even more concerned. It was Gabriel who answered, "His parents have asked him to stay on at his home. At least for now."

"But it's nearly the end of term. Can he really afford to miss school?"

"I don't think he has a choice," Miles said through pinched lips.

Gabriel said what we were all thinking. "The police believe he might have killed that young woman."

"But why? Why him more than anybody else?" I'd done the timeline myself. It seemed to me that everybody had left the room or been on their own at one time or another. Any of them could have killed Pamela.

"He received a phone call from her. And then he left the room and was gone for—" Gabriel rubbed his forehead. "Those dinners. I really shouldn't drink so much."

Miles nodded. "We've all got the same problem. We all saw him leave, and no one saw him come back. But he had to be gone at least twenty minutes."

Gabriel asked, "Is twenty minutes really enough time to kill someone?"

Carlos and Hester shared a glance tinged with smugness. Then Hester said in a soft voice, "You'd be surprised."

Wow. It really didn't look very good for Alex. He'd just gone to the top of my list of suspects too, and I was trying really hard not to come to any conclusions too quickly. As I had discovered from bitter experience, the minute you were convinced of someone's guilt, your mind spent all its efforts trying to prove your theory correct.

Far better to keep an open mind. Believe everyone was guilty and then eliminate the suspects one by one. Trouble was, I hadn't yet been able to take anyone off my list. If only I could get back into that house. I had a feeling that if I focused, I might be able to get a sense of what had happened in that billiard room. Maybe if Pamela hadn't passed all the way over, she'd even be able to get me some kind of a message. Somehow I had to let her know that I wanted to help solve her murder.

CHAPTER 12

$\mathcal{I}$ said, "I'd really like to visit Alex and let him know that I don't blame him for my friend's death. Maybe he's got some kind of information that would help us clear his name."

I didn't know whether Pamela had let on that we'd been more enemies than friends, or at least that had been true on my side of the equation. Hopefully, as far as Alex knew, we'd been dear friends who had rekindled our acquaintance. Then it made a lot more sense for me to barge into his house and ask a bunch of nosy questions.

Miles seemed quite enthusiastic about my idea. "Yes. That's an excellent plan, Lucy. I was thinking it might be good to visit him too. I can take his books down for him. At least he can do some studying while he's under house arrest."

"The police didn't do that, surely?"

"No. His parents."

He'd said he would take Alex's books to him. Did that mean he had a way into Alex's room here at Cardinal College? I told him I thought that was a fantastic idea and perhaps we could go down together. Gabriel decided that he'd like to come too. I could tell that Hester was dying to come along, but she had no earthly reason to be invited. Thank goodness. A surly teenager of a vampire was the last thing I needed when I was trying to solve a murder.

As we were all walking out of the pub, I said quietly to Miles, "Do you really have a way to get into Alex's room?"

He looked at me. "Yes. He keeps a key hidden. I do too. Sometimes it's convenient."

I didn't inquire too deeply as to what was convenient about having keys to each other's rooms. I looked at him. "You remember when we solved that murder during *A Midsummer Night's Dream?*"

He shuddered. "Don't even talk to me about that terrible time. If it hadn't been for you, Lucy, I really think I might have been blamed. I could be in jail even now."

I didn't want to boast, but I thought so too. I let that sink in. "I do have some talents in the area of solving crime. I know it's unorthodox, but do you think I could go with you when you get Alex's books from his dorm room?"

I could see him struggling with the right thing to do and, well, the right thing to do. Finally, he said, "All right. Just don't tell anyone."

I couldn't imagine I'd ever tell anyone about snooping into an undergraduate's room. Detective Inspector Ian Chisholm would have my head. Rafe would remind me that I was barging into the personal space of a possible murderer, and anyone else would just think I was a nosy snoop. I was a nosy snoop, but I didn't particularly want to share that information too far and wide.

The next morning, I said good morning to the porter—

who knew me by now, I'd been there so often—told him I was going to see Miles, and he let me through. Miles had an overnight bag already packed and said aloud, even though there was nobody in the corridor, "I'll just go pick up Alex's books then." I nodded and followed him along the hall. We got into the room, and while he went straight to the desk, I simply stood there for a moment looking around.

I didn't know what I was looking for. I had no idea whether Alex had had anything to do with Pamela's death or whether she'd even been here. I tried to let my witch self take over, the part of me that was full of intuition and strange powers.

Miles was a bit of a distraction, picking up books and flipping through papers, but I forced myself to push him out of my consciousness. I focused and looked around the room again, more slowly. "Pamela," I said silently, "were you here?"

Almost immediately, I knew that she had been. It was like a slight scent left behind when a woman wearing perfume leaves the room. Alex's dorm room was one of the most luxurious I'd ever seen, with a double bed, heavy tapestry curtains over the beautiful old windows, a desk under the window, a couple of easy chairs, and even a full en suite bathroom, usually unheard of.

I slipped into it while Miles was packing up a few things. I knew that if I was going to find traces of Pamela anywhere, it would be in here. I shut the door behind me and let him think I was going to the bathroom and quickly opened all the drawers and the cabinet.

Again, I caught an elusive sense of her but nothing that would help me.

The room I needed to get into wasn't Alex's. It was hers.

I bit my lip. How to manage it?

I came out, and Miles had a handful of books and a file of papers. "Okay, this should be it."

As we left, I asked Miles if he knew where Pam's room was. He looked at me over Alex's study materials. "Vaguely, but if she had a key hidden, I don't know where it is."

I sent him my cheekiest grin. Pulled one of the bobby pins from my hair. "Give me five minutes with this and a lock, and I'll have us inside."

"Won't the police object?"

"They'll have finished with her room by now," I said, as though I had a clue. However, because Miles pretty much owed me his life as well as believing I was a bona fide detective, he went along with my summation.

"All right. But I will hide cravenly in the stairwell while you break and enter. I can't afford to be sent down."

"Understood." I was delighted he wasn't going to be standing there looking over my shoulder because I wasn't going to use a bobby pin to open the room, obviously. I'd be using magic.

He led me to another floor and down a long hallway. He slowed and began to look from side to side at the doors, all of which looked alike. "It's around here, somewhere," he said vaguely.

Once more, I let my intuition lead the way. It was ridiculously easy to discover which room was hers. Having disliked her so much in life, her remaining energy hit me like a bad electric shock. I stopped and tapped softly on the door. "This one," I said.

There was no police tape stretched across the entrance, nothing to prevent a person going in if they had a way to do so. Miles was as good as his word and said he'd wait for me downstairs. "Unless you need me?"

"No." He looked very relieved. I was also relieved. I didn't want him with me for this bit of snooping.

A quick glance up and down showed the corridor still empty.

I flexed my fingers like a thief or a piano player, even though I'd be using my magic and not my fingers. I wished for Margaret Twigg, my witch mentor, but we'd been practicing a lot of spells lately, and I'd managed to both lock and unlock my own flat, car and shop. This shouldn't be too difficult.

What was hampering me was feeling that this was wrong. I had to get past it.

I breathed in slowly, then out. Felt the crackling negative energy begin to recede.

To open this lock let my wish be the key.

So I will, so mote it be.

I turned the door handle, and a bit to my surprise, it opened. I almost wondered if it had been locked at all. Of course, brilliant detective that I was, I'd never even turned the knob before attempting to open the door by magic.

I slipped inside and shut the door behind me, locking it by mechanical means rather than magical. Then I stood inside her room, my back to the door. I was immediately struck by the wrongness of her death. She'd had no warning, no time to prepare, and the sense of a young life cut off was apparent from her to-do list hanging on a bulletin board above the desk in her room.

I could see where her laptop had been. There were cords leading nowhere and the rectangular spot where her laptop had obviously sat. No doubt the police had the computer. Likewise, her trash can was empty. The police had gone through it, perhaps even taken the contents away.

What was left was just sad. I studied the list of tasks she would never complete. I read them and then snapped a picture with my phone.

She'd planned to attend an art premiere in London next week. I wondered whether that was for her coursework or for personal enjoyment.

There was a paper on Renaissance Perspective she'd never hand in.

The most interesting thing on the corkboard, however, was an article about the three missing paintings stolen from the college. Could Rafe be right? Was it possible that she was somehow involved in art theft?

Having snuck into her dorm room without permission, I had no compunction in going through the drawers of her desk. The police had already been through them and, I suspected, had taken most of the contents.

I found a few catalogs of art shows. I flipped through them, finding inventories for art shows and auctions that had already taken place. Stuffed into the middle of them, something that had obviously been overlooked by the police, was an envelope she'd used as a bookmark. Inside the envelope was her investment account statement, and the amount invested was eye-popping. Confirming, once again, that Pamela had not needed money.

I went through the rest of the room swiftly. Her bathroom contained high-end cosmetics as I would've expected, and her wardrobe contained exactly the kind of casual clothes that cost an absolute fortune, similar to what she'd worn the first time she came into my shop.

I reached in and touched a silk blouse that was hanging. I said, "I'm sorry you met such a terrible end, Pamela. We had our differences, but if I can, I will find who ended your life. Travel safe. Blessed be."

I stood there for a moment, breathing her scent. Her clothes were ruthlessly well organized, like the battle dress they were. I reached for a stack of scarves and chose a black cashmere that held her scent. It was too bulky to push into my pocket, so I counted on Miles being as unobservant as most guys about fashion and looped it around my neck.

Having spoken those thoughts aloud, I felt calmer, clearer, and when I was once again in the corridor, locking her door behind me, the energy didn't feel quite so angry and jangled.

CHAPTER 13

*M*iles arrived just before ten the next morning for our trip to visit Alex. I wore jeans and a beautiful, periwinkle-blue sweater that Christopher Weaver had knit for me. I kept my hair simple, tied back and out of the way. We loaded up my little red car and headed to the manor house. Luckily, Miles had been there before and knew where it was, because I'd only been with William that one time and I didn't think I could have found it again on my own. And I really doubted that Sir Hugo Percival Brown's house was something you could look up on Google Maps.

As we drove out, Miles told me that he was having second thoughts about being part of the Gargoyles. "It sounded like good fun when I was first invited, but I don't think my liver can take much more of this." He sent me a sidelong glance. "Not to mention it's a bit sordid, being involved with a murder."

I completely understood how he felt. "These clubs seem so archaic and outdated to me. Do they really do you any good?"

"You wait and see, Lucy. The same drunken louts who were sitting around that dinner table the other night will run this country in a few years. According to my father, it's well worth belonging." Then he said in a posh, older man voice that was no doubt meant to imitate his father, "You cannot overestimate the importance of connections in business. Vital, son, vital."

I was trying to keep my eyes on the road, but still I turned to look at him, laughing a bit at his coarse rendition. "But Miles, you want to be an actor. You don't want to run a sugar company."

"There is that." He seemed restless being cooped up in my small car. He looked out the window, shifted around a bit, turned back to look at me. "Truth is, it's my sister who's really got the business brain. I expect I'll make such a mess of it all that Father will end up making her the chairman."

He didn't sound devastated at the thought of being replaced by his younger sister, and I started to laugh. "Miles, you are not fooling me. I've seen you act. You're planning to act incompetent, aren't you? You don't have any intention of following in your father's footsteps."

His grin was entirely too charming. "You know me too well, Lucy. And yes. That's exactly my plan."

Miles had come close to his big break in theater less than a year ago. He deserved a second chance at the spotlight. Maybe he'd never do more than regional theater or bit parts in television shows and movies, but he could also end up as a big star. I thought he'd never be truly happy until he'd given his dream a try. I felt altogether better to know that he was planning exactly that, even if it did involve deceiving his father.

We were talking about movies we'd both seen and sharing our opinions, and it was nice to talk and laugh, and forget about murder, for the rest of our journey. But soon enough, we were pulling into the drive of the manor house, and the good feeling began to ebb.

This was a crime scene. A police van was parked in the drive. Even worse was a black, late-model Tesla. A car I knew all too well. "Oh no," I said under my breath.

"What's wrong?"

"Nothing," I said with false cheer. "I forgot to tell Violet about an order, that's all. I'll call her later."

We got out, and Miles shouldered the bag of study materials he'd brought for Alex. We trod up the front path, and he rang the bell. The door was opened by Mrs. Briggs, who seemed delighted to see us. "Lucy. How nice to see you again. And Miles, Alex will be pleased to see some friends. Come in."

We'd barely gotten inside when a very elegant-looking older woman, with stylish blond hair and a trim, athletic figure, came out of the dining room. Unlike Mrs. Briggs, she did not look delighted to see us. "Miles. Kind of you to bring Alexander his books. Not that he's likely to use them."

Miles looked a bit taken aback at her coldness. "Hello. I hope this isn't a bad time."

"I never recall a worse one."

What could either of us say to that? She looked me over as though he might have dragged me in the door by mistake. "No, that's fine. It's just that the house seems overrun with people today." She sighed heavily. "I'm going to have to get the billiard table recovered. And we just had that new felt put on."

It was an act of will for me not to gape at the woman. She acted like a murdered girl in her house was an inconvenience. An annoying housekeeping matter, like finding a mouse in the pantry.

I looked at Mrs. Briggs, and she was very studiously holding the placid smile on her face. I had a feeling she had worked hard on perfecting that expression and it would take a lot to shift it when her mistress was around.

Mrs. Briggs said, "You've caught us at a bit of a bad moment. But I know Alex will be very pleased to see you." She seemed to hesitate for a moment and then said, "Why don't you come back to the kitchen?" Oh, yes, please. I'd be so much more happy in the servants' quarters. Besides, perhaps if I was in the kitchen, I'd be less likely to run into...

"Lucy?"

Damn. I tried to look innocent as I turned to the man coming out of the lounge across the hall from the dining room. "Rafe. What are you doing here?"

Obviously he was looking at me like that should have been his line.

Luckily, Alex came running lightly down the stairs. I thought he looked tired. Possibly hungover. He needed a shave, and his hair could definitely use a comb. He'd gone beyond stylishly disheveled to just plain disheveled. Still, he did his best to assume his usual devil-may-care, cheeky grin. "Hey, mate," he said to Miles. When he looked at me, he wasn't quite as dismissive as his mother but not far off. "And you're the waitress from the other night."

I smiled at him sweetly. "I am."

Miles held up the bag of books.

He looked pleased. "Yeah. Good. Why don't you come upstairs?"

Mrs. Briggs said, "I'll bring you up some tea. Do you want some sandwiches?"

I'd have said no thank you, but Alex said, "Yeah, that'd be great. Thanks, Mrs. B."

I had to admit I was delighted to be getting a glimpse of upstairs. I followed the two guys up the stairs and pretended I didn't notice two very cold eyes burning into my back.

Alex had most of the top floor of the house. A huge bedroom, his own lounge, which included a massive television and all sorts of gaming equipment and computers and boy stuff, another smaller room that contained workout equipment and a desk that didn't look as though it got a lot of use, and a large, modern bathroom.

We all sat in the TV room. I admired the antique fireplace and the high ceilings and the beautiful windows that looked out on the green and peaceful fields of Oxfordshire. There were sheep grazing, and a line of trees hid what was probably a view of the motorway. But looking out that window, I bet that view hadn't changed much in the last two hundred years.

"How are you holding up?" Miles asked as soon as we were settled.

Alex slumped back in a chair that was obviously his favorite. "Bloody awful," he said. "I swear if my dad wasn't who he is, I'd be in jail by now."

"Surely it's not as bad as that?" I asked.

He glanced at me and back to Miles and then seemed to accept that I was part of this too. He said, "Oh, it's worse."

"Is it because Pamela phoned you during dinner?" I asked.

He shook his head. "She sent a text. She told me to meet her at our usual spot."

"What time was this?"

I got the feeling he'd asked and answered these questions so many times that he didn't even have to think. He simply pulled out his cell phone, clicked a couple of buttons and pushed it toward me.

Unlike fuzzy human memories, the cell phone let me know exactly what time he'd received that text. It had come in at nine thirty-seven, and it simply said, "Babes. Meet me at the usual spot." And a couple of kissy emojis.

"Where did you meet her?"

"The stables. There's a flat there that no one ever uses. We'd been there a few times. I went there to meet her, but she never showed up."

Or so he claimed. We all knew that she'd been killed around that time. What if she had shown up?

"Dad's hiring me a criminal defense attorney," Alex said. He said it with a sort of angry bravado, but I could see the fear behind his pose.

"Blimey," Miles said. "Do you think you need one?"

Alex shrugged. But he wasn't fooling anyone. He was scared stiff. "How do I know? The police definitely want to stitch me up for it."

I still thought that he was the most likely murderer, but I was determined to keep an open mind. "When she didn't show up, what did you do?"

He glared at me. "I waited for her. Why would she text me to meet her if she didn't want to meet? What kind of a stupid prank is that?" He looked annoyed that Pamela had somehow dragged him into her murder. In that moment, he reminded me a lot of his mother.

"How long did you wait for her?"

He shrugged. "I don't know. Fifteen minutes? Maybe twenty?"

I remembered again how wasted they'd all been. Time probably didn't mean a lot. "Did you see anything? If you didn't kill her, somebody must have."

He looked a bit embarrassed. "I might have fallen asleep for a few minutes."

I was about to press him further when there was a most unwelcome interruption. Rafe walked in.

CHAPTER 14

I glanced up at him and could see that he didn't look to be in a very friendly mood. He looked cold, forbidding, and to someone who knew him as well as I did, furious. *Great.*

"Lucy." Oh, his voice was so pleasant and smooth. Only I could hear the bite. "Do you have a minute?"

Of course, I wanted to be childish and chicken and tell him I didn't. I was far too busy hanging out with Miles and Alex, but I knew it was pointless. He'd find a way to get me out of here, so I said, as brightly as I could, "Sure."

I excused myself and followed Rafe out of the room. As soon as they couldn't see us, he grabbed my hand and pulled me down the hall and into the office that Alex used. He shut the door. "What are you doing here?" He really did sound furious. But I knew Rafe. He got like that when he was worried about me. Still, as I had told him about a hundred times before, I could handle myself. "I came with Miles. Pamela was my—okay, she wasn't my friend, but it was my fault that she was even here that night. I'm trying to find out what happened to her."

"I don't think so."

"What do you mean you don't think so?"

"Never mind that now. You need to leave. You are socializing with the main suspect in a murder investigation. Might I remind you that a man who would kill one single female from Boston might well kill another one."

I glared at him. "I really don't think Pamela was killed because of her relationship status or where she was from."

"Why do you think she was killed?"

And wasn't this the question we'd been poking at for days now. "I don't know. That's one of the reasons why I'm here. And why are you here?"

He looked down his nose at me. He could do cold disapproval better than anyone I knew. "I was invited."

"Lucky you."

"Hugo asked me to come today and provide moral support, I suppose. The police are still going over the crime scene."

"I know. I saw the police vehicles outside. What do we know?"

Rafe had connections all over the place, and one of my favorites was some inside source he had who could get him copies of autopsy reports, sometimes before the detectives had them. Usually he was most happy to share, but because he was annoyed with me, I could see him struggling with himself. Then finally he said, "She died of asphyxiation."

"So she was strangled?"

"Yes. And that belt was the murder weapon."

He looked at me, and I knew there was something he wasn't telling me. I'd known him long enough that I knew not to push. I stood there in silence and waited. Finally, he said, "Come with me."

He didn't give me any explanation, just opened the door and headed down the hall. Obviously, he assumed I would follow. I was tempted not to, but usually it was better if I did follow him. We'd been talking about the autopsy report, after all. What did he know? Teasing me like that was as good as putting a leash around my neck and hauling me behind him. He knew I'd follow him. And I did. I followed him all the way to the billiard room.

"Why are we here?"

"The forensics people finished in here about half an hour ago."

"You mean we can go in?"

He nodded. Then he opened the door and ushered for me to go ahead of him. I walked in. I could smell that slight, chemical scent that I'd come to associate with fingerprinting powder. The billiard table with its bright red felt gave me the creeps. But I forced myself to go near it. I walked around the whole table slowly. Pamela had spent her last moments here. She'd died here. There ought to be something left. Rafe didn't say anything. He simply watched me out of those icy blue-gray eyes.

I'd felt Pamela so strongly in her dorm room yesterday. Even in Alex's dorm room, I'd experienced a sense of her essence. So far, in this room, I was coming up blank.

No doubt it was Rafe throwing me off. I centered myself. Focused not on the vampire who dominated the room but on the woman who'd died here. I took another tour around the room, silently calling on my former friend.

And I felt nothing.

Finally, I opened my eyes as the obvious truth struck home. "She didn't die here."

He nodded slowly, and I felt like I'd won a prize. "The police aren't certain, but they don't believe she died here either."

We stared at each other, the obvious question between us. If she hadn't died here, where had she died?

I went back upstairs and found Miles and Alex tucking into sandwiches and beer. They offered me a beer, but I stuck to sparkling water. I did have a sandwich though and found that they'd moved on from talking about the murder to talking about their studies. I needed to move the conversation back again though, and I didn't want to sound like I was a police investigator. I hoped that, seeing that the weight of guilt and horror must be heavy on Alex's mind, he'd bring it up again. Or Miles would.

So I listened through Homer and something that I thought might be mathematics, and then Miles said, "Oh, I don't know if you need this or if it's useful, but I found this in my pocket."

He pulled out the map he'd used to get to the wine bottles in the wine cellar.

Alex looked at it and shuddered. "Chuck it away. I don't want it."

I wanted it. But I wasn't going to say anything. I watched as Miles scrunched the paper into a ball and chucked it into the wastepaper basket in the corner.

Alex stared into his beer for a minute. I could have kissed Miles. The sight of that map brought Alex's attention back to the murder. "I can't believe it. I can't believe she's dead."

My patience had paid off. I asked, "How did she come to be here for your dinner anyway?"

He glanced up at me as though it was my fault. "She was your friend. You know why she was here."

"But was it your idea that she be a server that night? Or was it hers?"

"It was hers. I thought she was joking. See, my dad was so anxious that there not be any hot women here that he was hiring some bird out of a knitting shop to wait on us. I told Pamela for a laugh, and then she said she knew you and wouldn't it be funny for her to show up and do some serving." He sipped his beer. "Like I said, I thought she was having a laugh."

As the "bird out of a knitting shop," I wasn't very amused.

"I never believed she'd actually do it, because..." He stopped himself and dove back into his beer again.

"Because she'd been here before, hadn't she?"

He looked at me now like I might be a witch or something. "How do you know that?"

I wasn't going to let on that he had a very chatty housekeeper in case I got Shannon Briggs into trouble. "I heard a rumor."

Once more, he got that sulky schoolboy look. "She was only having a bit of fun, planning to surprise me. Except my dad was here, and the whole thing ended in a great row. So, yeah, I didn't think she'd seriously come back into this house again. Not when she knew he'd be here."

She had to have a good reason. I wondered once again if she was somehow involved in art theft. As a former dealer, she'd been perfectly placed; then, an art student in Oxford. I began to wonder if it wasn't a title she was after but their priceless art collections.

I now knew that Pamela hadn't been killed in the billiards room but moved there after she was already dead. I bet the forensics people were now going over the stables where Alex had admitted going to meet with her. If they found she'd died there, not all the family money and connections could save him.

Sometimes, when I was practicing a new spell, Nyx would watch me, clearly worried I might set the flat on fire or something by accident. She'd have one eye on me and be ready to bolt out the open window at a moment's notice. That's how Alex watched me now. Finally he blurted, as though he couldn't stop the words, "I didn't kill her."

Unfortunately, mind-reading wasn't one of my talents, so I had no way to tell if that was the truth. I would have to rely on good, old-fashioned sleuthing techniques. Like asking a lot of nosy questions. I was becoming a master in the art of nosy questions.

"Did the other Gargoyles know that you were seeing her?"

He looked at Miles with his eyebrows raised. Miles shrugged. "I'd seen you with her. Didn't really know what the story was." I could have driven a truck through the pause between those two sentences. What Miles was saying seemed secondary to what he wasn't saying.

I had no time for innuendo. "You mean she wasn't the only one you'd seen Alex with?"

"I never said we were exclusive," Alex said, as though we were arguing. "If she thought different, that was on her."

No one said anything, and his color rose. If he'd said that to the police, he'd have put himself one step closer to a murder conviction.

CHAPTER 15

*T*hat night I called an emergency meeting of the vampire knitting club. Not everyone could make it, as even vampires tended to make plans, but Gran and Sylvia came, Rafe and Theodore were with them, and as I'd begun to think we were a small enough group that we could go up to my flat, Hester and Carlos came in from the street door.

"I'm so pleased you've called us together tonight, Lucy," Sylvia said. "I've been crocheting you a tunic. I want to check the fit." I was really happy that there was some knitting and crochet on tonight's agenda, because I was very much hoping somebody would help me untangle my knitting. Again.

Nyx wandered in from her favorite napping spot in my front window and ran to Rafe. Cats were usually so standoffish, but not Nyx. At least, not with Rafe. He picked her up and put her over his shoulder, and she snuggled happily against him.

Sylvia pulled out the tunic, and I sighed with pleasure. The color was somewhere between emerald and teal. She held it against me and nodded, looking pleased with herself.

"I thought this would be perfect with your coloring, and I was right."

I touched the lacy garment. "It's so pretty."

Gran came closer. "Pineapple stitch. What a lovely color. That will be perfect for spring."

"Yes, that's what I thought. I can't decide on whether to stop the tunic here"—she touched the waistband of my jeans —"or to go to mid-thigh." She and Gran stood back and cocked their heads, as though they were Dior and Givenchy and I was the model who got no say in the spring collection. I was trying to decide which one I'd wear more often when Sylvia said, "I'll make it in both lengths."

Thus making me very pleased I'd kept my mouth shut. I could wear the shorter one with jeans or a skirt, and the longer one would be perfect over leggings. Sylvia sat down and got her crochet work moving so quickly I had to look away before I got dizzy.

Gran pulled out the throw she was making for my couch upstairs. I'd chosen the pattern from one of the new magazines. It was a pretty design of Cotswolds roses and was intended to hang over the back of my couch, though I suspected we all knew it would end up as a cat blanket for Nyx.

I pulled out my tangle, and Gran immediately looked over. "Oh, love, whatever have you done?" I somewhat sheepishly handed over the mess, and she rapidly got to work.

I didn't feel as bad as I might have, since Hester was doing the same with Carlos, who was also struggling with his scarf.

Once we were all settled, Rafe and I caught them up on what we'd found out at the manor house, and then I asked Sylvia how she'd made out. She looked rather pleased with herself. "You were right, Lucy. Vikram is a beautiful young man. He reminds me so much of his grandfather."

"You've seen him?" She'd moved quickly.

She looked a bit like the cat that got the cream. "I took him for afternoon tea."

I couldn't even imagine. "Tell me you didn't share with him that you knew his great-grandfather? Like a hundred years ago?"

She looked at me reprovingly. "Lucy. Do you think I have no subtlety? I told him I was an old friend of the family. And he was too polite to pry."

I wasn't sure I liked that she'd taken Vikram to tea. He was so gorgeous, even I'd wanted to take a bite out of him. And I didn't have her cravings. "What did you two talk about?"

She fluttered her hands so her jewels sparkled. "What does one talk about at tea? His beautiful country. What I remembered of it. We talked about his studies. He's a lovely young man, excellent manners."

"And then you asked him about the murder?" Because that was nice teatime conversation.

"Not exactly. I told him I'd become a matchmaker."

For some reason, the hairs on the back of my neck began to stand up. "You did what?"

"Oh, yes. He's quite accustomed to it, you know, in his culture."

"And did you offer him a match?"

"Well, you did say that you liked the look of him, and I could tell he'd quite warmed to you." She spoke rather coyly and gave me a bit of a sidelong glance. She was up to something, but Rafe had been standing behind her and hadn't seen her face.

He made a sound almost like a growl. "You will not make a match with Lucy and anyone from the Gargoyle Club. Is that clear?"

As though he hadn't even spoken, she said, "If he'd pressed the matter, I had Violet in mind to present to him."

It was all I could do not to laugh. She'd set Rafe up so beautifully, and he'd fallen right into her trap. "Violet?"

"Of course. She comes from an excellent family. Naturally, I'd give her a very nice dowry."

"And was Prince Vikram interested?" I had no idea whether she'd lost her mind or was playing some deep game.

"He's already promised to a woman in India."

"Really?"

"Yes."

Theodore had been watching intently. He said, "If he'd been interested in Pamela or someone like her, that wouldn't look good to his wife-to-be, now would it?"

She met his gaze and nodded. "I'd wondered that myself, but it was clear that he'd never thought of Pamela that way. Unless he's a better actor than I am, which of course isn't possible. However, he did let slip one interesting piece of information."

"I'll bite. What was it?"

"I got him talking about the murder, which wasn't hard to do. Obviously, it was a rather dramatic occurrence. And, as I was an older woman and a friend of the family, he confided in me. He wondered if he should tell the police something."

She must have been a great actress. Her timing was brilliant. She had all of us leaning forward, hanging on her every word now.

"And what was that?" Rafe asked her silkily.

She twisted a gorgeous ruby ring on her finger, and I immediately knew, either through witch intuition or the good old women's kind, that Vikram's grandfather had given her that ring. "Vikram said he went to the bathroom on the night of the dinner. And he overheard an argument."

Nobody was going to do her the favor of asking who was arguing. We all just looked at her. Still, she let the dramatic pause lengthen and finally said, "It was between Jeremy Pantages and Alexander Percival Brown."

"About?" Okay, I could only be patient for so long.

"About Pamela. He says they had heated words."

"Did he recall what those heated words were?" It was Gran this time, pushing her friend to be a bit quicker in relating these stirring events.

"He couldn't be completely certain. And, although he didn't want to admit it to me, I suspect he was inebriated. But he confirmed it was a heated exchange, and he believed they were arguing about who should have Pamela."

Like she was a toy to be fought over. These guys were so entitled, I could hardly stand it. "Who won?"

"It seemed more like a heated exchange than any kind of a resolution was reached."

"They really do seem immature for their ages. I was surprised Pamela would be interested in Alex. Sure, he's gorgeous and loaded, but she didn't need the money." I thought again about the lengths she'd gone to for Alex. "She must have really wanted that title."

Rafe put down his knitting so it draped adorably over Nyx, who was curled up in his lap. "What title?"

"The title Alex will inherit when his father dies. That must be what she was after." That and a lot more millions.

He shook his head. "Hugo Percival Brown has a lifetime peerage. It will die with him."

I was so shocked, I dropped a stitch. Maybe a couple. Knitting and sleuthing did not go together in my hands. "You mean even if she married Alex, she'd never have been Lady Percival Brown?"

"No. Not unless Alex did something remarkable in his own right, and from what I've seen of that young man, I shouldn't think it's likely."

Theodore had brought along the Oxford newspaper. Naturally, Pamela's murder was front-page news. He passed it around, but only Gran took the time to read the article. I imagined the rest of us had already read it and there was nothing in the report that we didn't already know. There was a photograph though, and Gran sighed over it. "Such a pretty girl. What a sad end."

She reached the end of the article on page one and, as I had done, turned the newspaper a couple of pages to continue reading. Sylvia glanced over at the paper spread on Gran's lap and suddenly let out a strangled shriek.

We all looked at her. Even Gran looked up from what she was reading. "What is it? Did you see a clue that we all missed?"

But Sylvia wasn't looking at the article about the murder. She was looking at a headline next to that article. And there was a photograph. I put down my knitting very happily and came over to have a look. Sylvia pointed her finger at the picture, stabbing it in the newspaper. "They can't do this. You cannot improve on perfection."

When she finally stopped stabbing at the picture, I could

see that it was a movie still. The headline read, "*The Professor's Wife* to be remade. Filming to begin in Oxford."

I was slightly puzzled, but Gran obviously knew more than I did. "*The Professor's Wife.* That was one of your more famous pictures, wasn't it?"

"It was. And I was brilliant. That's why the film is a classic."

"Why do they always remake the good films?" Gran wanted to know. "There are so many bad films that could be improved upon."

"My thoughts exactly. I must see what I can do about this outrage."

I stared at her. "How do you think you could stop it?"

She struck a pose. "I hope I'm not nobody."

Well, in vampire circles she might be a big somebody, but in the world of the living, she didn't hold much sway.

We were all staring at her, and she must have realized the predicament she was in, for she slumped back in her chair. "All right, I can't personally get involved, but what about my estate? There must be something we can do to stop that film."

"Not unless you own the rights," Rafe said. As an antiquarian book expert, he probably knew a lot about book copyright, and presumably film copyright wasn't that different.

"I've got money. I'll hire the best attorneys. I will put a stop to this."

"No offense, my dear," Gran said to Sylvia, "but your movie was silent. Perhaps if they remake it with sound, it will be a completely different experience." She didn't say what probably all of us were thinking. Who watched silent movies anymore?

Maybe the odd cinephile, but going back to before the talkies was hard for anybody. I tended to agree with her. A version that included speaking parts was probably not a bad idea. Not that I'd ever heard of this famous movie anyway. I'd have to check it out.

Sylvia looked seriously annoyed, and she said, "One has standards. Who's to say this won't be some tawdry, cheap rendering of a story that was so beautiful in its time?"

I gave a gasp.

Sylvia turned to me, looking pleased. "You agree with me then."

"No. I mean I do. I guess. But you made me think. Lowering the standards. We've spent all this time focusing on the eight young Gargoyles. But what about the older ones?"

Rafe looked at me as though he was having trouble hearing me. "What are you talking about? You thought Lochlan Balfour was the murderer. He's by far the oldest Gargoyle who was at the dinner that night."

"Okay. I did. But then we quickly moved on. And ever since then, we've been concentrating on the eight guys downstairs. Mainly Alex."

"That's because they were the ones who knew Pamela, and Alex was obviously in a relationship with her, as casual as he may claim it was. It doesn't look good for him, Lucy."

I wasn't particularly bothered about Alex one way or the other. I thought he was an entitled twit, but if he hadn't killed Pamela, I didn't want to see him punished for it. "Here's what I'm thinking. What about his father?"

"You think Hugo killed Pamela?"

"I don't think anything. I'm just throwing out ideas here. But what if he didn't want to bring down the standards of the family? He was obviously a strict father, and that wife sure looked like a snob. In fact, if she'd been anywhere in the area, I'd have tried to pin the murder on her. She wouldn't want an American divorcee marrying her precious son. I mean, Pamela might have a lot of money, but they don't need money."

"So you're suggesting that Hugo Percival Brown murdered his son's friend because he thought the son was getting too close to her?"

"Well, maybe he knows more about the relationship than we do? Maybe Alex was more serious about her than he's letting on. This whole 'we were just having fun' thing might be a smokescreen."

He took his time answering. Finally, he shook his head. "The timing doesn't work. We were with Hugo when his wife telephoned."

Okay, I tried not to feel disappointed, because I wasn't trying to pin a murder on anyone who didn't deserve it. Still, I had liked my new theory. "It's that whole chivalry thing that I keep coming back to and the way the body was displayed. If chivalry is about saving people from bad things, then perhaps he was trying to save his son from a bad marriage."

"He's a very ambitious man, is Hugo. I wouldn't necessarily put murder past him if it would serve his purposes, but he's proved himself more ruthless in the business world than in his personal life."

"And you said he had an alibi?"

"Yes. His wife phoned at ten o'clock, remember."

"Are you sure it was his wife?"

"Yes. He'd warned us she would. They always speak at ten when they're apart. I have extremely good hearing, Lucy. I recognized her voice. She was telling him that she was thinking about firing her hairdresser, if you must know. She feels, now his salon is so famous—thanks, apparently, to her—that he's become too controlling."

Okay, that totally sounded like wife and husband conversation. And exactly the sort of thing that Alex's mother would focus on. "And how long was the conversation?"

"Well, he left the room to speak with her. And returned I would say about twenty or twenty-five minutes later."

"You're right. The timing doesn't work."

His eyes glinted with amusement. "You sound disappointed."

"Are you sure it's not Lochlan Balfour?" I was quite willing to move on and try out different perpetrators.

"It could be Lochlan Balfour. As you say, he was the only one who was actually a Knight of the Garter. But I can't imagine why he'd display her body that way. And I can't find a plausible motive."

"But you were separated for a time?"

"We were. While Hugo was speaking to his wife, Lochlan and Henry went to look at the Picasso at the end of the hall." He seemed like there was more to say, so I waited. "Henry's convinced it's a fake and wanted Lochlan's opinion."

"I feel like everyone was running all over the place that night. Don't people ever sit down and eat dinner properly anymore?"

"Well, it was a very long dinner. And, of course, Lochlan and I weren't as interested in the food as some of the others."

"Right." He took the term food sensitivities to new heights. I remembered something and pulled a crumpled paper out of my jeans pocket. "Miles left this behind. It's the map showing him how to get to the wine that night."

Everyone was looking at me as though waiting for the rest of the sentence. Waiting for me to finish my idea. It was still fuzzy and unformed. I wasn't even sure if it made any sense. "I know that Miles and Charles both went to the wine cellar to get the wine. I just wonder if we should time how long that takes."

Theodore looked at me curiously. "You suspect Miles?"

"Not really. But that Charles, I didn't like him at all. He struck me as a cocky womanizer."

Theodore gave a kind of snarky laugh. "I think you could say that about all the members of the Gargoyle Club." He didn't look at Rafe, but he didn't have to. I tried to hide my smirk.

Rafe replied anyway, "In my day, we were a little better behaved."

I doubted very much that was true, but I didn't want to get sidetracked. I showed them all the printout. "I hear this wine cellar is pretty intense."

None of them looked very impressed with it. I supposed being their age and vampires, they'd seen cellars, wine and otherwise, that were a lot more grand than this. "Well, it looked impressive to me. Anyway, I still think it's worth going in there and tracing their steps and timing how long it takes. You see, Charles didn't walk back with Miles. He went out the downstairs door."

Rafe put up his hands. Nyx headbutted his forearm until he went back to stroking her. "Again, what was his motive to murder Pamela?"

"I don't know. But if the timing works, then maybe we can start looking into him more carefully."

Rafe seemed to be thinking. "I could get into that wine cellar."

"Rafe, I don't want to go breaking in and sneaking around in the night."

"No. In the daytime. Hugo and I were talking about wines. He offered to sell me a case of Château Margaux."

"Really? He has a better wine cellar than you?"

He looked at me as though half my brain might be missing. "Of course not. However, he did manage to buy up a collection before I'd even heard of it."

How I prevented myself from rolling my eyes, I will never know. "Okay. You get us in there. I'll bring my phone and time us."

I knew he didn't want me to come, but what could he say? It was my idea. Finally, he said, "All right. But you do not leave my side. Until the murderer's caught, that is a very dangerous place."

I agreed. I didn't want to wander around a dark, dusty cellar by myself anyway. I didn't have a death wish. Rafe might be a lot of things, but he was an excellent protector.

CHAPTER 16

*V*iolet complained that I was leaving her alone to run the store again, but she didn't sound very sorry to have the place to herself. She tended to slack off when I wasn't around, reading the newest knitting magazines instead of putting them on display, and between customers, I suspected her of playing on her phone instead of cleaning and re-stocking shelves. However, she was good with the customers and she was an excellent knitter, plus, family. Since she was also a witch, I didn't have to hide my powers around her, which was a real bonus.

Rafe came to pick me up, and we drove to the Percival Brown residence. "How are you going to explain me being here?" I asked him as we purred along in the black Tesla.

"You leave that to me. Your only job is to keep your mouth shut and do as I say."

This time nothing in the world could prevent me from rolling my eyes. He might be able to see me out of his super vampire peripheral vision, but I really didn't care. "You have noticed that in the last century, women have been allowed to own property, vote, have our own opinions. We're allowed to work outside the home. The world is such a different place than in your time."

"As you keep telling me." He didn't sound like it was an improvement, but I suspected he was winding me up so I refused to engage in a fruitless argument.

Instead, I watched the scenery go by. It was a beautiful, spring day, and the fields were green, the lambs were adorable puffs of white staying close to their mothers, and wild bluebells were beginning to bloom. We passed ancient pubs, new housing developments and the odd historic monument.

Around noon, we pulled up in front of the Percival Brown residence, and I was pleased to see that there were no police cars this time.

Rafe rang the doorbell, and Briggs, the butler, answered. He seemed pleased to see us. He was the most likable butler. "Rafe, what a pleasant surprise. And Lucy. Welcome."

"I hope it isn't too much of a surprise. Hugo has a case of wine for me."

"Yes, he left instructions. Unfortunately, he's had to go into town today. But he told me to give you the key to the wine cellar. I can take you down there if you like, but he said you know your way."

"I do. Lucy's trying to learn about wine storage, so I brought her along." Oh, that was thinking on his feet. I could see that Briggs was wondering what I was doing here. Since he associated me with catering rather than knitting, the excuse was a good one, and it immediately cleared the puzzlement from the butler's brow.

"Would you like some refreshments before you head down to the cellar? Tea? Sandwiches?"

"No, thank you. We won't take up too much of your time."

I surreptitiously pulled out my phone, and as we passed the dining room, I put on the timer.

I followed Rafe down to the cellar. He unlocked the gated entrance and opened it for us, then turned on the light switch. The bulbs were dim and dusty, but at least they cast enough light for us to find our way into the labyrinth before us.

Rafe and I walked in. Immediately I felt the change in atmosphere. It was cool and still. There was some kind of ventilation coming from somewhere, because it didn't smell dank or damp. I looked around, and all I saw was rows of bottles of wine. It was like a bookshop, only instead of being crowded with books, it was loaded with bottles and bottles. Each squared-off section had the kind of wine, and the year, and it looked like the number of bottles. Most of them were dusty with age. "This is so cool," I said.

I pulled out the map, and we made our way to the spot where the wine for the dinner had come from.

"He's very deep into burgundy," Rafe murmured as we went past vintages that went back to the 1930s.

As I moved deeper into the wine cellar, a strange feeling began to press upon me. It was like sadness, darkness. I felt like my heart was beating too fast. Was I getting claustrophobic? I lost interest in reading labels and dates. I wanted to get out of here and fast. We found the wine from the dinner party. I could see the space where the wine had come from. Nothing seemed out of the ordinary to me. I glanced at Rafe. "Can we go now? This place is giving me the creeps."

But he was standing very still, and he lifted his head a little and sniffed the air, like a police dog on a scent.

"Do you sense anything different?" he asked me. He might be pretty dismissive of me a lot of the time, but he definitely took my witch talents seriously. Well, more seriously anyway, now that I was actually learning to use my talents.

"I feel darkness and almost a sense of claustrophobia," I admitted.

He said, "Turn off that timer. We can roughly double it if we're working out the timing for the boys getting back to the dining room from here. But let's take a look around."

I didn't really want to. I wanted to get out of there. But I knew that my fear was senseless. I was completely safe with Rafe, and the chances that a manor house that had been standing for two hundred years would suddenly decide to fall in on us was extremely unlikely. "It took us seven minutes to get here, so the return trip would take fourteen minutes." Rafe was already moving, so I took a deep breath, centered myself, said a quick spell of protection and followed him. "Can you smell something?" I asked him.

"It's very faint. But I think that waitress was in here."

"Well, she was supposed to come and get the wine, but it ended up being Miles and Charles who fetched it."

We walked down to the end of one corridor of the cellar. I was facing a bank of champagnes. Who had a whole wall of champagne? We turned at the bottom and began to head up the other way, and the feeling in my chest grew heavier and heavier. It wasn't claustrophobia. What I was sensing was death. We moved on, and I stopped. "Here. Something terrible happened here." I felt nearly sick. And my skin was growing clammy. I forced myself to breathe and focus, and I looked around carefully. But this corridor looked exactly like the last one. Rows and rows of dusty bottles. And then something caught my eye. Down toward the bottom near the ground. I dropped to my knees.

"What is it?" Rafe asked.

"Look," I said, pointing. He crouched down beside me, and only then could he see what I had noticed. An area where the dust had been rubbed off some of the bottles.

He nodded. "Her scent is a little stronger here, too."

"Do you think she was killed here?"

"Yes. Do you?"

I nodded. But also felt very confused. "What does this mean?" I asked Rafe.

"I think it means that you should be very careful being alone with your friend Miles."

"No." I hated the idea of Miles being a killer. He'd already been falsely accused once.

The bottles in the wine cellar had been placed cork toward the wall so that the round bottoms were all that I could see. Rows and rows of them. Not only were they covered with dust but also cobwebs. But there in that one section near the bottom, it was as though someone had taken a duster and wiped them clean. I believed this was where Pamela had died. Rafe seemed to agree with me. I was surprised that he hadn't been able to more acutely smell her death, but of course, in a strangling death, there hadn't been any blood. I felt as though my own throat were constricting as I swallowed. "But Miles and Charles were together. You're not suggesting they both did it, are you?"

He looked as puzzled as I felt. "I have no idea. I don't

know why the two of them together would kill her or why either of them separately might have."

"I saw an old Hitchcock movie once about people who plotted a death just to see if they could do it." I dredged up the memory. "*Rope*. I think that's what it's called."

Rafe looked at me with his eyebrows slightly raised. Right. Movies weren't his thing, though I was attempting to improve his cultural education. I'd made him sit through *Star Wars* and some of my other favorite movies, but we'd never watched Hitchcock. I'd be adding some of them to the list.

"In *Rope,* they were college students too. They had approached murder as an intellectual exercise." I tried to imagine Miles plotting cold-blooded murder and it wouldn't come. He wanted to be an actor. Not a killer.

But Charles? I could see him turning unpleasant if he didn't get what he wanted. And he clearly thought of himself as quite the ladies' man. Could Pamela have given him the brush-off? Even if she had, I couldn't imagine him killing her, unless it was a drunken accident.

"So now we know that she was killed here and then moved into the billiards room, what does that change?" Rafe was looking around at the bottles as though he were either hoping one of them would break open and give him the answer, or perhaps he was browsing the collection.

I looked around me too. "I think this changes everything."

That brought his attention back to me. "How so?"

I was going on instinct and a kind of hunch that wasn't even fully formed. The last thing I was ready to do was share it. I only knew one thing. "We have to get hold of Ian."

Rafe never looked very happy when the subject of Detective Inspector Ian Chisholm came up. Probably because he knew I had dated Ian a few times. The romance hadn't really gone anywhere, but I think Rafe always worried that one day we might pick it up again. What he had to offer and what Ian Chisholm had to offer were so very, very different. I liked Ian, but my secret powers would always be between us. I didn't have to hide my true self from Rafe. What I felt for him was deep and complicated, and I couldn't see how it could end well. Still, there was no doubt that we were more than friends.

"Let's get out of this cold cellar," I said, walking out. It felt even more oppressive bringing this load of confused emotions into an already confined, dusty cellar. I felt like I needed to get some air on every level.

The first thing I did when we got out of the cellar was to call Ian on my cell phone. He answered right away. "Lucy. What can I do for you?"

"Where are you?"

"I'm just pulling into Hugo Percival Brown's manor house. Can I call you back?"

"No. I'm here. Your timing could not be more perfect."

He didn't sound so delighted that I was at the manor house. "What are you doing there?" His voice was sharp and accusing. "You're not snooping, are you?"

What other possible reason could I have for being here? Of course, I was snooping. Still, I wasn't going to give myself up that easily to a sharp-eyed detective. "I'm visiting Alex."

"You are now friends with Alexander Percival Brown?"

"Yes." No, but hopefully he wouldn't find that out. "I came here with Miles Thompson. You know Miles." Since I actually was friends with Miles, or at least had some kind of history with him, Ian had to back off. "Be careful, Lucy. A murder happened there, and the murderer is still at large."

A chill crept down my arms. "I know. That's what I want to talk to you about. Can you meet us at the entrance to the wine cellar?"

"Us?"

I rolled my eyes even though he couldn't see me. "Rafe Crosyer is with me."

"Of course he is." Said with complete sarcasm.

Oh, this was nice. Now I was going to be stuck in the middle of a tug-of-war, with two men pulling at me emotionally. I didn't have the time or energy to cope.

However, as grumpy as he'd sounded when he hung up, Ian arrived within five minutes. He must have come straight in the front door and come down to see what I had found. One thing about Ian, he might be irritable with me, but he'd known me long enough that if I wanted to show him something, he knew it was probably worth looking at.

He was wearing his usual suit, with white shirt and tie. He gave Rafe a curt nod, which was returned in kind, and then said, "What's all this about, Lucy?"

I couldn't tell him about my witchy senses, and I certainly couldn't tell him about Rafe's vampire senses, so I'd come up with the best I could. Lucy the super sleuth. "I think I found something. Follow me."

Rafe said he'd take his case of wine to the car and meet me out there. No doubt he believed Ian would be more likely to listen to my theory that Pamela had died here if Rafe wasn't around. No doubt he was right.

I led Ian back into the wine cellar, past the section where the wine from the other night was stored, and he paused.

"Isn't this where you want to be?" So he'd traced Miles and Charles's footsteps too and no doubt timed the return trip.

"No. What I want to show you is around here."

Our footsteps scuffed along the paved cellar floor as he followed without comment. I led him to the spot where I was almost certain Pamela had been killed. Ian looked around, looked at me, and then I realized what a super weak clue this was that I was offering him. If he couldn't feel the psychic energy that I was picking up on, all he was going to find was a patch where some dust had been wiped off some bottles. A hundred things could have done it. Somebody coming in here with a broom, an animal brushing by—what had I been thinking? Still, I knew that this was the spot where Pamela's life had ended. I had to help Ian come to that same conclusion. I squatted down and pointed to the area where the dust had been wiped off the bottles. "I think that Pamela may have died here."

As I had feared, he looked at me like I was a few bottles short of a wine cellar. "Based on what?"

Based on my witch's powers, which he didn't know about. I tried to sound convincing. "Isn't it possible? This is the only area where dust has been wiped off the bottles. Look here and here. Imagine I was being strangled." I put my own hands to my throat and mimed pushing back against one side of the row of bottles and over to the other and then falling to the ground. I wasn't much of an actor, but I could make the marks on the bottles match.

"A number of things could have wiped the dust off these bottles. Is that all that you've got?"

"Call it a hunch. At least investigate."

He put the flashlight on his phone, which wasn't exactly

calling in the forensics team, and, squatting down, ran the light over the area. He was about to get up and I knew I was going to get some scathingly dismissive comment when he stopped. And muttered something.

"What is it?"

Was he actually going to believe me?

Almost to himself, he said, "The forensics team found traces of red dust on her clothes. We thought it was from the stables, but we haven't been able to match it. Maybe it's red dust from the bricks."

When I looked closer, I could see what he meant. While she'd rubbed dust off the bottles as she was falling, she would have also rubbed against the crumbling, old, red brick that was part of the cellar.

I felt a rush of elation. Mostly about being believed. "So you think I'm right?"

He looked at me with a strangely intent expression. "I think you have remarkable hunches." He didn't say it like it was a compliment, almost as though there was some kind of con going on. Of course, there was, but he was a man of evidence and science. Of rational explanations and clues that built up a case that was then proved in court. Saying that I was a witch who felt death? That was not going to go down well with Detective Inspector Ian Chisholm.

So I tried to wave off his words. "Call it women's intuition."

"I don't believe in women's intuition."

Not wishing to hang around so he could interrogate me any further about my brilliant intuition, I said, "Well, I'll let you keep investigating."

As I left the cellar, I could feel him watching me.

CHAPTER 17

*a*s we drew near Oxford, Rafe turned to me and said, "What are you thinking, Lucy?"

He said this because I'd been quiet for most of the journey. And Rafe knew me well enough to know that this was unusual behavior. He tended more to the strong, silent type while I was closer to the chatterbox end of the scale. But my mind was running in a million directions at once. And unfortunately, everywhere it went, it seemed to hit a dead end.

"It all comes back to the timing," I said. "Every time I think I have it figured out, the sequence of events doesn't work. Or I get the timing to make sense, but my suspect has no reason to kill Pam."

"Murderers lie, as well, which doesn't help."

He was right about that, of course. "Let's get the vampire knitting club together tonight. I want to pull every single piece of evidence we have, every story we've heard, everything we can think of. Let's put it in one place and see if we can get a picture to emerge."

"That's an excellent idea. Do you mind if I bring Lochlan?"

"Isn't he a suspect?"

"He had no reason at all to kill that woman. What he does have is a fresh perspective."

I supposed having one more gorgeous vampire wasn't too much of a hardship, so I agreed Rafe's houseguest could join the knitting club this evening.

"I've been thinking about Pamela's ex-husband."

"What about him?"

"He's a well-known property developer in Boston. Very rich and connected."

"And?"

"I think I'm going to give him a call."

"Do you think he'll speak to you?"

"No idea, but maybe he has some ideas on why she was killed."

Rafe offered to take me for lunch, but I told him I needed to get back to the shop. It was true, but I also wanted to do some thinking and make that call. As he was dropping me off, he turned to me. "I'd rather know you're on the phone to someone who's miles away than consorting with possible killers."

Frankly, I felt the same way.

I found William in the shop talking to Violet. I said hello and wondered if he had another catering gig he wanted us to help him with, but he seemed at a loss for a reason to be in Cardinal Woolsey's. He stammered that he'd been passing by and wanted to make sure Vi was okay after the shock of the other night.

I glanced from one to the other and thought they both

looked like they were up to something. I was so busy thinking murder and motives that it took me a few seconds before I smelled romance in the air, which had so much sweeter a scent than death and murder. But wait, I smelled something else as well, when William reached into a bag at his feet and brought out a wrapped baguette. "Vi and I had ours, but I brought you some lunch."

"Definitely the way to my heart," I joked, taking the wrapped sandwich. Though I wondered if it was Violet's heart he was interested in.

"Don't rush off," I said. "I've got some work to do upstairs."

And I left them to it. Nyx followed me up to my flat. Maybe the flirting was getting on her nerves. I wasn't certain how I felt about this possible pairing. Would those two be good for each other? On the positive side, William knew all about Violet being a witch, and she knew all about Rafe. On the negative, I wasn't certain they fit together. But maybe that was natural fear on my part because I liked them both so much and didn't want to suffer the consequences if the relationship didn't work out.

I wondered if Rafe knew and what he thought.

Once we were in my flat above the shop, I made us both lunch. A can of high-end tuna for my fussy familiar, and I got out a plate and unwrapped the baguette William had given me. I immediately checked out the contents. Oh, yum. Brie, with thin slices of apple. I munched my way through while I thought about Pamela, the wine cellar and how that shifted things.

When I was done, I placed another call to Sarah in Boston, the one who had known Pamela. And from her I got the name and contact information for Pamela's ex-husband.

I didn't relish calling a man who was divorced from Pamela. If I was bitter, I couldn't imagine how he felt about her, but I had an idea. I had no idea if it made any sense, but like Ian had said, my hunches were pretty good.

Pamela's ex-husband wasn't the kind of man who answered his own phone. I reached an assistant and then managed to get through to his personal assistant, and when I gave my name, she insisted on knowing what it was about. If I wanted to talk to the husband, I was going to have to be honest. "It's about his ex-wife's death."

"Mr. Forbes has already spoken with the Oxford police," she informed me coolly.

"I know." I didn't, but it made sense that they'd called him. I wondered if I could have saved myself this call. But I could talk to him in a way that the police couldn't. I didn't want to pull the "I was a friend of his ex-wife" card because I hadn't been Pamela's friend and I didn't want to lie. "Please. It's important."

"I'll see if he's available," she said in a tone that suggested hell would be frozen over long before I'd be talking to Pamela's ex. But to my surprise and no doubt to hers, in a very short period of time a man said, "This is Conrad Forbes. How can I help you?"

He had a no-nonsense voice and, I suspected, very little time to waste on me. I had to plead my case and do it quickly. Which, of course, made me completely blithery and tongue-tied. "Hello. I'm sorry to bother you. My name is Lucy Swift. I knew Pamela in Oxford."

"Yes. And how can I help you?" No warmth. If anything,

he sounded colder than his personal assistant had. No doubt his time was worth about a billion dollars an hour, so every second was valuable. I cut straight to the chase. "I need to ask you why your marriage broke up."

"And why is that your business?"

"Because I'm trying to solve her murder." I thought he'd just hang up on me if I didn't give him a reason to help me. "She betrayed me, too. Back in high school. I'm going to take a wild guess that Pamela was unfaithful to you."

His laugh was low and bitter. "You did know her. As I told the police, I won't miss Pamela, and I certainly won't miss the massive alimony check every month. But I didn't kill her." There was a pause, and I could feel there was more coming. "And I didn't hire anyone to do it either."

I hadn't even thought of a hitman. He must really have hated her.

"Who did she leave you for?"

"No idea."

"But you're certain there was someone?"

"If you knew Pamela, then you knew that she was always looking for the next bigger thing. The bigger fish to land."

I didn't know this man, but I was positive he hadn't passively let her go. "And who was a bigger fish than you? Come on. You must have hired a private investigator." He was definitely the kind who kept PIs in business. I had no idea whether he'd done such a thing, but a guy like that? With both his ego and his money on the line? Even as I said the words, I was positive he must have done so. And the fact that he didn't end the call was all the answer I needed.

"That's personal."

I heard his pain and shamelessly used it to push. "But it

could help solve her murder. You loved her once, enough to marry her. Don't you want to at least know who killed her? And why?"

In the pause, I heard his breathing change. He likely wasn't aware that his breaths had become short and jerky. "She was clever and hid her tracks well. I did have her followed but never successfully. She had to have help covering her tracks so thoroughly. Whoever she was meeting had a high level of security." I got the feeling he thought he was a pretty giant fish. "Now, if you'll excuse me, I've got a meeting."

Darn it. I thanked him for talking to me and asked him to call me if he thought of anything else. But I knew he wouldn't. If he was like me, he just wanted to forget about that woman who'd caused him so much trouble. I was about to hang up when he said, almost as though he thought I was gone and he was speaking to himself, "I never should have given her that damn gallery."

As I ended the call, I looked at Nyx, who was happily enjoying a post-lunch snooze, curled up on the couch with a shaft of sunlight making her sleek coat glow. "And what did he mean by that?" I asked her.

She shifted so her nose was tucked more deeply under her paw.

I SPENT the afternoon making up orders and letting Vi deal with the customers. I preferred being tucked away in the back room so that when I lost track of what I was doing and stared into space, I wouldn't upset the paying public.

Because I was seriously distracted. Art. Between Pamela's gallery and taking her degree in art history and the way she'd been studying the paintings in the Percival Brown residence, there was a connection. But what?

While I packed up orders and wrote out shipping labels, I kept wondering. I was driving myself crazy. Why couldn't I let this go? There were competent police on it, and I had a business to run and sweaters to knit. Why did I keep pushing myself into police business?

But I knew the answer. I hadn't liked her. She had treated me badly. But Pamela had been my friend once. And she was a woman like me, an American in England, without a lot of friends here. If I was killed, I would want to know that there'd be someone like me trying to find out what had happened.

Besides, maybe it would finally give me some closure.

So I continued to puzzle over Pamela's death while Vi took care of the customers. Violet was good-humored and more than usually helpful, which made me wonder if there was something between her and William to put her in such a good mood. However, she didn't tell me, and I didn't pry. At this stage, I didn't want to know.

Vi had gone home and I'd just closed the shop when Sylvia appeared with Gran. They had the look they always got when they had a new sweater for me to model. The bag in Sylvia's hands was a bit of a giveaway too.

I never got tired of their gifts, especially when they were made by someone of good taste and fashion sense. Like Sylvia.

Eagerly, I pulled out the tunic sweater she'd been crocheting for me. I wouldn't have known a pineapple stitch from a pineapple, but the result was gorgeous, lacy and breezy, and the color reminded me of swimming in the Mediterranean beaches of Egypt while visiting my parents.

"I love it," I cried. It was too see-through to wear on its own, but I told them I had a white T-shirt I could wear beneath it.

"You could," Sylvia agreed unenthusiastically, then put her hand into the bag I'd believed was now empty and pulled out a silk cami in a paler shade of turquoise.

"Perfect."

"And try it with those nice silver hoop earrings you have," she instructed. "And I'll do your hair."

I felt puzzled. "Is there an occasion?"

She looked taken aback. "Does one need an occasion to look one's best?"

CHAPTER 18

Once more, at ten o'clock that night, we convened. I had my hair styled a la Sylvia in a messy updo that looked like it took thirty seconds to achieve but had taken the better part of an hour. It had been fun as we three chatted and caught up, talking about everything except murder. Sylvia had also done my makeup, and she was right—the silver hoops looked perfect with my new sweater.

Finally, Gran had clasped a silver bracelet around my wrist. "I bought this for you in Ireland, my love." I'd seen the same design on rings, two hands entwined around a heart.

"It's beautiful."

"It's a claddagh. For love, loyalty and friendship. All of which I have for you."

I hugged them both, and then we went down together for the impromptu vampire knitting club meeting. I didn't bother taking my knitting. I knew I wouldn't be able to concentrate.

As the group began to gather, I got a few compliments on my new sweater, and I happily showed off my new bracelet as well. Gran said, "I was disappointed not to find a shop to rent in Ballydehag, but perhaps I'm not quite ready to leave Oxford."

"We'll keep looking," Sylvia assured her. Because, as hard as it was, we were going to have to get Gran out of Oxford before she ran into an old friend when I wasn't around with my trusty forgetting spell.

Lochlan and Rafe arrived together. Lochlan thanked me for inviting him as though this was a great treat.

Rafe made the introductions, though most of the vampires already knew the Irish vamp.

"Right," Lochlan said, rubbing his pale hands together. "Let's catch a murderer."

That was as good a way to start our meeting as any. I told them about my phone conversation and how Pam's ex had hired a PI who never found evidence of an affair. Theodore, as a private investigator himself, seemed unimpressed with his American colleague's work. I got the feeling that he was fairly certain if he'd been on the case, he would have uncovered plenty of evidence. "So that's a dead end, then."

"Except that we know that she moved from her husband to somebody who must have been richer and maybe even titled. She wouldn't have left her husband if she didn't think she was onto a good thing," I said.

"Do you think that's what brought her to England?" Gran asked.

"I don't know. But I doubt she came purely to get a degree," I said. "So whoever she left her husband for, what happened to him? Did they break up? Or did she follow him to England?" I told them about seeing that Instagram photo of her and Jeremy at the Henley Regatta last July. "Is that who brought her to England? Was it someone else?"

I looked at Theodore. "What do you think?"

He looked quite pleased to be asked. "The trail is cold, of course. But I do like a challenge."

"There isn't time for you to go to North America, though. Do you have contacts there?"

"Lucy, I have contacts everywhere."

The vampire network never failed to impress me. There were underground roots connecting clusters of vampires all over the world. And they seemed to have an amazing intelligence-gathering network.

"Okay. See what you can find out."

Then I related that final comment, that Conrad Forbes wished he hadn't bought Pamela an art gallery.

"That must be where Pamela met the man she began her affair with," Lochlan said, glancing around. "Surely?"

Sylvia, who had been inspired by a Dolce & Gabbana crocheted dress on the Milan runway, was once more busy with her crochet hook. However, she stopped the rapid movement and glanced up. "Isn't Harvard in Boston?"

"Yes."

She appeared troubled. Finally, she said, "Prince Vikram told me he spent last summer in Boston with friends. No doubt it's a coincidence, but I felt I should mention it."

"What do you think, Lucy?" Theodore asked me.

Like Sylvia, I hated to think of that delightful man somehow being involved with Pamela or, even worse, in her death. "I don't know. I didn't see any interaction between them at all the night of the dinner." I turned to Rafe. "Did you?"

He shook his head.

Theodore reported that Pamela's tutor did have a book

coming out about Renaissance painting, but Pamela had never offered to hold a party for him. No surprise there. Theodore also said he doubted the man was involved in art theft since he was in his eighties and suffering from macular degeneration.

"You mean he's going blind?" Dr. Weaver asked.

"Yes. So he'd have no use for paintings."

I looked around the room. "We're missing something. What is it?"

Every one of us looked frustrated. Sylvia said, "If only Pamela could speak to us."

I had an idea. One that had been growing on me all evening. "Maybe she can."

Sylvia turned to me. "You can speak with the dead now? Your witch abilities have improved."

"No, I can't commune with the dead. I'm not that good a witch. But I have a way that Pamela could get a message to her killer." And that got everyone's attention.

I said, "Theodore, can you manipulate a photograph?"

Theodore looked quite perturbed at the question. "Why on earth would I do that?"

"Because we need proof. And we don't have any."

Theodore looked as stern as his baby face would allow him to. "Lucy, are you suggesting that I, a licensed private investigator, tamper with evidence?"

I made a sort of a cringing face. "Not tamper with evidence, exactly. More like invent the possibility."

"Certainly not." He looked like I'd really disappointed him. "I could lose my license."

I thought he'd lose it a lot faster if whatever governing body there was discovered he was undead.

Into the slightly uncomfortable silence, Hester said, "I can do it."

We all turned to look at Hester. "You can?"

"Don't look so surprised. What else am I supposed to do with my time?" She let out a huge sigh. "I'm so bored. So yes, I play on the computer."

"And you can manipulate photos?" Carlos asked her.

"Yeah."

"That's so cool." He sounded quite enthusiastic, which perked her right up. But being with Carlos always perked her up. She'd come so far from that droopy, mournful teenager constantly dressed in draping black. Now she wore tight jeans and a sweater that was dark purple. Okay, it wasn't a big jump from all black, but it was a step forward.

However, I was more interested in her photo manipulation abilities than her fashion sense right now. "So if I wanted you to create a photo with two people in it, you could do that?"

She rolled her eyes. "Easy."

Theodore muttered to the effect that he wanted nothing to do with my antics and wouldn't be responsible for the consequences of my rash behavior. I understood his concerns and assured him that I would use this fake evidence to provoke a confession. I wouldn't use it to trap an innocent person.

He didn't look relieved. "I don't like it. I don't like it at all."

I didn't love it either. But even less did I want to see a guilty person go unpunished.

I told Hester exactly what I wanted her to do, and Carlos volunteered to be her helper, which ensured that the job would get done.

The next thing I had to do was get Miles on board with a plan that was only just beginning to form in my head.

Rafe had been watching me. "Lucy? What are you plotting?"

He knew me far too well. "It might not work, but I have an idea."

"Is there anything I can do to help?"

I almost beamed at him. After Theodore telling me off for concocting evidence, it was so nice to have someone be completely supportive. I nodded. "As a matter of fact, there is." I told him what I wanted him to do.

I felt as excited as if I'd nailed a new spell. Better, in fact, because if I was right, I'd used deductive reasoning and not magic to find the answer and hopefully catch a killer.

CHAPTER 19

The next day, I caught up with Miles. He looked pleased to see me but preoccupied. However, I caught his full attention when I announced, "I have an amateur acting gig for you."

"You're a theater director now? What happened to your knitting shop?"

"Very funny. No. This is a one-night-only performance. But it will be a very important one. I want you to play a part. My intent is to provoke a confession from the person who killed Pamela."

He looked astonished. "You know who killed her?"

"I think so."

"Who is it?"

I shook my head. "The thing is, we don't have enough evidence. I want you to enact a part, intended to provoke a scene that will hopefully lead to unveiling the murderer."

"I've always wanted to play Hamlet," he said, striking a pose.

"Hamlet?"

"Lucy, you sorely lack a classical education. At the center of Hamlet, there's a play within the play, where Hamlet has a play put on specially to mimic his uncle's murder of his father."

Whatever worked to get Miles on board. "Okay. You can be Hamlet." I looked at him sideways. "But no iambic pentameter."

He laughed at me. "I promise."

Then I told him everything he had to do. When I left, he looked more cheerful than I'd seen him in ages. That guy really needed to get back on stage.

Next I had to get Detective Inspector Ian Chisholm on board. I knew this was going to be the most difficult part of my plan. However, Ian had known me long enough that I thought he'd come to trust me, at least to a certain extent. The thing was, as a bona fide police detective, he was very limited in what he could do. I didn't even tell him the way I was manufacturing evidence because I knew that would be the end of any cooperation from him or his department. So I merely said that I had an idea and I wanted to bring everybody back together in that same house and see if we could get to the bottom of what had really happened.

"I've known you a long time now, Lucy. When you get that tone in your voice, I have learned to distrust it."

He wasn't a detective for nothing. "I know. But have I ever led you astray?"

He made a funny noise. "All the time." He didn't expand on what he meant, and I didn't push.

"Anyway," I said breezily, "if you could come to the manor at seven o'clock tomorrow night, I think it would be worth your while."

"This would be unofficially, of course."

"Of course. But if you had some officers in the area, that might be very useful."

There was a long pause when I wondered how I'd ever come up with a plan B when I barely had a plan A, but finally he agreed.

Okay, now I had all my players. The one thing I didn't have yet was the cooperation of Hugo Percival Brown and his family. Naturally, I hadn't told anyone that yet. This was where Rafe came in.

Some things are just better done face-to-face. I'm a big fan of phones and texts and instant messaging, but when I need someone to do something, and it's a little bit out there, I've always found that meeting face-to-face is the best. Besides, I liked being with Rafe.

The shop was just closing when he came in. I knew before he entered when Nyx, who'd been sound asleep in my front window, curled up in adorable repose in a basket of multicolored wools, suddenly raised her head and her eyes opened wide, as though a particularly succulent mouse had run in front of her. There was no mouse. It was Rafe coming down the street. Maybe I wasn't a cat, but I definitely stood up and took notice too. I hastened away from the window before he could see me. Nyx had no such qualms. She was out of her basket, stretching her back and grooming herself before he arrived.

The door opened, and the cheerful chimes sent out their song of welcome. Before I could reach him, Nyx meowed, and he immediately headed to the front window and scooped her up. She curled herself against his chest and looked at me through her green-gold eyes as though to say, "Ha. He definitely likes me the best."

"Thanks for coming by," I told him.

"I'm intrigued, Lucy. You're up to something, and for once, I don't know what it is."

Score one for me. "Probably best you don't know everything because I'm pretty scared I'm going to screw up. Here's what I want you to do for me. Can you call Hugo and arrange for everyone from the Gargoyles who was there the night Pamela died to return tomorrow night at seven p.m.?"

"That's exactly when we met the last time. What are you planning? Another dinner?"

"Not exactly. But I want to do a walk-through of what happened. When. Who was where and what they were doing."

"Lucy, we've been through this a hundred times." He pointed to the back room. "There's a whiteboard in there at this moment with people and times and comings and goings. You know the police have been doing something similar. And they have training and resources that we don't."

"I know. But I have an idea. A hunch, if you like. But I can't find any proof. So—"

"You're going on a fishing expedition?" He didn't sound accusatory so much as intrigued. That was exactly what I was doing. I nodded.

"You know, you'll only get one chance. If that. It won't be easy for me to talk Hugo into letting us all back into his home." He made a wry face. "Even worse, his wife won't be in London this weekend. She's even more protective of their privacy than her husband is."

Good. I was really glad the wife was going to be there. She didn't know it yet, but she would be playing a pivotal role.

"I want her to be there."

His eyebrows rose at that. "She was in London the night of the murder. You don't think she had something to do with this, do you?"

"I think she does, yes." It was too complicated and very much like a sweater I was attempting to knit. I had the whole design in my mind, and I could see it laid out perfectly, every stitch neatly executed, me in control of the whole design, when I knew perfectly well that anything I tried to knit usually ended up a tangled mess. However, my vampire knitters always helped me straighten out my knitting messes, and I was confident that they could also help me make sense of this tangle of clues and lies. Because I was absolutely certain of one thing. The reason that nothing was making sense was because someone was lying. And I suspected that someone had murdered Pamela.

"Why gargoyles?" I asked him.

He appeared startled. "I beg your pardon?"

I'd been thinking about this for a while now. "Why do you call yourselves gargoyles? It's a dinner club. It seems like an odd choice of a title."

He appeared to be looking back in time and enjoying some sort of private joke. "Ah, well, you have to remember that the dining club was set up in Victorian times. There was a gothic revival going on. I suspect the name was meant partly in jest."

"Because gargoyles are really just a fancy name for gutters?" I'd done a bit of researching on the internet.

"Yes. You're correct, Lucy. Gargoyles do serve a useful

purpose. They take rainwater off the roof and keep it off the masonry so that the walls last longer. There have been gargoyles since Greek times. I believe the Temple of Zeus featured lion-headed gargoyles. And, as you've no doubt seen, they're all over Oxford. Humorous ones, terrifying ones, just plain peculiar faces leer at you from all sorts of colleges and buildings. There's also the idea that their ugly faces are meant to frighten away evil. Keeping those inside safe."

"So it sort of goes back to chivalry again?"

"In a way, yes. But I doubt the name was ever meant to be taken too seriously. People at a dining club tend to get a little carried away with gluttony and perhaps imbibing a little too much wine. It can lead to the best of men putting their worst faces forward."

Which we had certainly seen recently. "Well, I need you to get all the Gargoyles together. Can you do that?"

"I think I can manage it."

"I need Lochlan Balfour there as well."

"He's still here. That won't be a problem."

Maybe in naming the club the Gargoyles, it encouraged people to act like monsters. They'd have been better to call the dining club the Little Lambs. The Delicate Blossoms. Something less dangerous to society, in any case.

Saturday came and, even though I was busy at the shop all day, I never forgot what was waiting for me that evening. Was it possible I was wrong? Even worse, was it possible I was right? I had a theory, and my instinct told me that I was on the right track, but if I was wrong, I was going to make a phenomenal fool of myself and, by association, everyone who had helped me.

However, everything was arranged. Rafe had managed to

get all the players to agree to return to the scene of the crime. Ian Chisholm had agreed to be part of it. I couldn't pull back now if I wanted to.

I closed the store at five as usual. Well, I tried to close the store at five as usual, but there was an older woman who just couldn't decide between the yellow wool and the green for her unborn grandchild. I appreciated that this was an important moment for her, and she was so excited to be a new grandmother. But really, yellow? Green? Finally, I suggested that she buy both and make two blankets. This satisfied her, and at ten after five, I was able to shut the shop. I went straight upstairs. Nyx was more strict about store hours than I was, and she had already retreated upstairs and was sound asleep on the couch. "I'm glad you're still here," I said to her. "I need you."

She opened one eye, regarded me sleepily, then closed it again. My familiar is nothing if not obedient.

I went ahead anyway, preparing myself. I brought out the candles and put them in a circle. I showered and changed into clean clothes. I fetched the black cashmere scarf I'd brought from Pamela's final home. I cast my circle. And then, practicing my newly found powers, I ignited the candles by pointing at them. This still thrilled me every time it worked. Also, being able to do that basic magic, to create fire, gave me confidence. I might not be the greatest witch on the planet, but I was getting better. I was learning.

I breathed in and breathed out. I focused on cleansing my mind of all the clutter of the day, everything except Pamela and her murder. I could hear Margaret Twigg's voice in my head. "Focus, Lucy. Magic is about focus and intent. Where your intent lies, your magic follows."

I had looked in my family grimoire for truth spells, but sometimes I found I did just as well or better creating my own spells. I sat quietly, feeling Nyx watching me. Pamela's scarf was in my hand. The candles flickered around me. For a moment, I thought about the face of the gargoyle.

One who is hiding in darkness, may he reveal himself today,
Let his real self show clear
Let me operate without fear
He has taken a life and for that he must pay
So I will, so mote it be.

I closed the circle then, and feeling calmer and clearer, I got ready for the evening.

I dressed simply, in jeans and a white shirt with a woolen blazer, and tied around my neck was Pamela's scarf. I also wore the silver bracelet Gran had given me, feeling myself wrapped in her love and care. Then I went down and waited outside. Rafe was right on time. He took one look at me and said, "Are you nervous?"

He could always pick up on my emotions. "I'm so nervous, I feel sick." Also, my heart was beating against my rib cage so I imagined he could probably hear it. His hearing was extraordinary.

He reached out and took my hand in his. "Your motives are pure. That's what matters. If you can help solve a murder, then you've done us all a service. If not, you've tried."

That was comforting in an oddly frustrating way. I did not want to try and fail. I wanted to succeed. But, even for me, I was winging it here. I had never, ever manufactured evidence before. Hester had come through for me, and I had a couple of photographs in my handbag that would, I hoped, be dynamite.

However, I knew that on its own, a doctored photo wouldn't be enough. All I could do was to nudge things forward in the right direction. If I was wrong, if my entire theory was a bunch of garbage, I wouldn't change the outcome. If I was right, we just might catch a killer.

As we purred through the darkening countryside, I went through everything again in my mind. This was it. As Rafe had warned me, I had one chance to get into the Percival Brown's home. One chance. I'd better not blow it.

No pressure then.

WHEN WE ARRIVED at the front door, Hugo Percival Brown opened it himself. He did not appear very welcoming. There was a furrow between his brows. "You said it was important, Rafe. I hope you know what you're doing."

Rafe had been around a lot longer than Hugo Percival Brown, and if everything he told me about his very long previous life was true, he'd been up against a lot tougher characters than this one. He pulled himself up to his full height, which was like six feet three or something, and said, "I think it's going to be an interesting evening. Thank you very much for accommodating us." Hugo might be a bazillionaire and looked up to by everyone from high school kids to leaders of government, but he didn't impress Rafe, I could tell. Hugo could tell it too. He nodded curtly and stepped back, letting us both in.

We were the first, as I had hoped we would be. Within fifteen minutes, everyone who had been at the original dinner where Pamela had died was back again. They hadn't worn their Gargoyle costumes, which kind of made it all the more surreal. Without the fancy coats and waistcoats, the eight undergrads just looked like that. Eight undergrads forced to spend the evening at one of their parents' homes instead of being out on a Saturday night.

And the older men just looked like four dads. Mrs. Percival Brown was the only one who seemed to have dressed for the occasion. She wore a gorgeous black dress that showed off a stunning figure. Her frosted hair was in an elegant chignon, and diamond drops glittered at her ears and throat. Her high heels strangely reminded me of the ones that Pamela had worn the night she was killed. However, her expression was cold and distant. She might be forced to entertain all of us, but she made it clear that she wasn't going to enjoy it.

Rafe went to her immediately and kissed her on both cheeks, European style. "Genevieve," he murmured. "You're looking lovely, as always."

He managed to thaw her by a scant degree.

I had given Rafe instructions on how I wanted everybody positioned. It was obvious that Hugo would listen to him when he would never listen to someone like me. In fact, I'd deliberately echoed the black and white outfit I'd worn last week, as a subtle reminder that I was of little importance, of so little threat I was nearly invisible.

So, as people gathered, Rafe asked them to go into the dining room and take the same seats that they had occupied at the beginning of the evening that Pamela had died. This put Hugo Percival Brown at the head of the table and his son at the foot. Everyone then took the places they'd had before.

Genevieve Percival Brown said, "Well, I wasn't here, so I'll be upstairs if anyone needs me."

I sent Rafe an urgent look, but it wasn't necessary. He said, "I'd be very grateful if you'd stay. There are a couple of questions I have for you."

She glanced up at DI Chisholm, who had arrived and was sitting in the corner, quietly watching. He nodded.

"Very well," she said crisply. The words bounced like hail. She didn't pull up a seat at the table, however. She chose to sit outside the dining circle, in a wingback chair beside the buffet.

William Thresher stood just inside the door, with Violet beside him. And I positioned myself on the other side of the doorway.

Rafe stood. He had a commanding presence anyway and completely took control of the room. "Thank you very much to everyone for coming. Especially to Detective Inspector Ian Chisholm, who is here not in an official capacity but because I have asked him to come."

That wasn't true, I had asked Ian to come, but Ian didn't correct Rafe, merely nodded. He might be here in an unofficial capacity, but I knew there were officers ready to close in in a minute if we got lucky tonight. Honestly, I was so nervous I could barely breathe.

I realized now that it wasn't me who'd look completely stupid if this whole thing turned out wrong. It was Rafe who had accepted the responsibility. He glanced over at me in that moment as though he knew I was thinking about him and gave just a slight smile. It was a ghost of the smile he kept just for me. And I suddenly felt so much better. Maybe this wouldn't work, but maybe it would. At the very least, we were trying to find justice. I touched Pamela's scarf. That had to count for something.

Rafe said, "I feel responsible in some way for the young woman's death the other night. It was I who suggested William Thresher as a caterer. And through him, Pamela was hired as a waitress. Therefore, since I feel some personal responsibility for that young woman's welfare, I wanted to bring everyone together one more time and see if we could begin to understand what happened."

"She was killed. That's evident to all of us," Hugo said in some irritation. "The police have interviewed all of us, ad nauseam, and I've had to take valuable time away from my business. So unless you've got something new to bring to the table," and here he spread his open hand over the gleaming mahogany dining table, "then I suggest you are wasting everyone's time."

Wow. It wasn't often anyone ever spoke to Rafe that way. In fact, I couldn't think of a single time I'd seen it happen. Hugo didn't know, as I did, what Rafe was capable of. For just a second, I saw his face darken and felt danger, and then he clamped down on the hidden part of his nature and urbanity returned.

"But thank you anyway for indulging us. Let's begin right away and then we can all waste as little time as necessary."

Just the fact that Hugo Percival Brown thought time taken from his business because of a murder that had occurred in his own house was wasted made me like him even less. Not that I was a big fan of his to begin with. Or his entitled son, who sat at the other end of the table, his gaze on a portrait of his mother that hung on the dining room wall as though he'd never seen it before.

"The police have established the time of death as being between ten p.m. and ten forty-five. Correct, DI Chisholm?"

"Correct."

Mrs. Percival Brown now stood up. "For goodness' sake, Rafe. We all know that. If I'm to sit through the tedious recital of a dinner party I didn't attend, I'm going to need a drink."

No one said a word. She glanced at her husband as though he might oblige, but he didn't even look up. Finally, with a muttered exclamation, she clipped her way over on her high heels to a beautiful cabinet at the far end of the room. She took a crystal tumbler and filled it with amber liquid. Whiskey, I imagined.

She was like a one-woman play. She didn't offer anyone else a drink, and as she poured her own, there was complete silence. Even from where I was sitting on the other side of the room, I could hear liquid pour into the glass. That's how silent it was. And she clipped her way back and sat down.

Rafe continued, "It's not the timing that's so confusing. It's the motive. Why would someone in this house want to kill Pamela Forbes? A waitress hired for the evening?"

Hugo spoke up again. "We don't know that she was killed by someone who was here that night. There's always the possibility it was an outsider. The doors weren't secured; our staff had the night off. I have made that clear to the police."

"Indulge me."

It was clear that Hugo Percival Brown was accustomed to being the dominant force in the room. Rafe had taken the spotlight off him and in his own dining room, and he didn't like it. However, he must have realized we were all here now and it would be simpler for him just to let Rafe continue than to keep interrupting him. He said nothing, and after a moment, Rafe continued.

"William Thresher is an excellent caterer."

What? He was totally going off script here, and while William looked startled, he also looked gratified at the praise. "He also times things to precision. William? Can you go through the schedule of when your various dishes were served?"

"Oh, for heaven's sake," Genevieve muttered. "Will we be given the recipes too?"

William did as he was asked and walked us through every course, from the appetizers that went on the table at seven-thirty through the dessert. While it was kind of boring, what happened was that everyone in the room who'd been probably rigid with nerves began to relax.

"All right," Rafe said. "Thank you, William. Now let's go over the critical time. Alex, you asked Pamela to get the key to the cellar from your father and fetch more wine."

The young man of the house looked sullen at being put in the spotlight. "That's right."

"Because eight bottles of three-thousand-pound Bordeaux weren't enough." This was his mother, already on her second glass of whiskey.

"Genevieve, please," Hugo said. I got the feeling these two argued frequently about their son. "I told him they could have as much as they wanted. It was a special night. It was bad enough the boys had to come here for the evening. I wanted them to have a good time." Of course, the reason the boys had had to come to his house for the evening was that every respectable place in Oxford was closed to them. However, nobody called him on it.

"What time did you ask Pamela to fetch more wine from the cellar?"

"I don't know," Alex said. "I wasn't watching the clock."

"I was watching the clock," William said. "Lucy came in and told me, and it was about twenty minutes past nine."

Rafe continued, "Pamela came upstairs and asked you for the key," he said to Hugo, who, now that this procedure was underway, seemed resigned.

He nodded. "I went down, opened the cellar up for her. I showed her where the bottles were, and then I left her."

"And no one saw Pamela alive after that."

"That's not true," Winnie suddenly piped up. "She texted you, Alex."

Everyone turned to look at Alex, who was squirming under the scrutiny. He looked both angry and ill. If I was nervous, I couldn't imagine how he was feeling, as suspect number one in a murder case. "I didn't see her." He said it angrily, as though he'd said these words many times before and was tired of being disbelieved.

"But you did leave the table when you received that text."

He nodded sullenly. "She said she wanted to meet me. I've told the police all this. I went to meet her in the stables, the old stables, but she wasn't there."

"So you say," Jeremy Pantages said icily.

Alex half rose and glared at him, but before he could say anything, Rafe said, "And what time did you get that text?"

He heaved a huge sigh as though this was an enormous inconvenience, but he pulled out his phone. He pulled up the text and showed Rafe. Rafe read it aloud to all of us. "'Babes. Meet me at the usual spot.' That was received at nine thirty-seven p.m."

Alex reddened. He took his phone back. "I've told you, she never showed up."

Rafe said, "So, if you never saw her, and you're telling the truth—"

"I am."

"Then Pamela was never seen alive again after she left the room to fetch the wine."

There was general puzzlement. Charles said, "But she wasn't killed until later. Somebody must have seen her. She didn't turn up in the billiard room until closer to eleven, when we found her...like that."

"That's right. And that's what the murderer has been wanting us to think all along. But she wasn't killed in the billiards room. She was already dead when she was put there. I have a theory." He didn't have the theory. I had the theory, but it was nice to hear my theory offered with such confidence and so forcefully when I was feeling a lot less confident.

"My theory is that the murderer sent that text."

It would be wrong to say there was a collective gasp around the table, but there was definitely an electric buzz that went silently through the room. DI Chisholm hadn't told the Percival Browns or anyone else, as far as I knew, outside of the police about the new evidence.

"What?" This was Charles.

DI Chisolm now spoke up. "He's right. Pamela wasn't killed in the billiards room. Her body was moved postmortem."

Alex turned to Miles and Charles. "I sent you fellows down to check on her. And it was ages before you came back."

Charles said, "I didn't have anything to do with this. Don't try to pin it on me. She was seen talking to Jeremy outside, and Vickie heard you two arguing."

Prince Vikram didn't look thrilled to be dragged into the middle of this fight, but he nodded.

Alex said to Jeremy, "It was you, wasn't it? I came back when I couldn't find Pam, and you weren't in the dining room, either."

"I was in the toilet."

"I don't believe you. You were furious that she dumped you for me. You were jealous. You couldn't have her to yourself, so you killed her."

Jeremy then retaliated, "And you were furious that she still fancied me. I think you did meet her. You killed her in the stables. Then moved the body to the billiards room."

Wow. This was taking an interesting turn.

Alex got out of his chair so fast, the ornately carved chair fell over. He had an ugly look on his face and began to round the table with murder in his eyes as he headed toward Jeremy. Lochlan Balfour was so quick, he'd grabbed Alex before he'd gone three feet. He held him with one hand, picked up the chair with the other, and pushed him bodily into it. And he stood beside Alex with his arms crossed, like a jailor.

"I am getting a headache," Mrs. Percival Brown said in an angry tone.

CHAPTER 20

The atmosphere was thick with distrust, dislike and an undercurrent of fear. By this point, we all realized that a murderer was in this room.

And the murderer knew the truth was closing in. I could feel it.

And then Miles began to cry. At first he dropped his head into his hands. I could see the manly attempt he made to prevent himself from making a fool of himself in front of his friends. My heart went out to him. Then a sound, half groan, half sob, escaped him.

Gabriel asked, "Miles? Are you okay? Do you need some water?"

He shook his head and then scrubbed his face with his hands. Mortified at his womanly tears. "She was my friend."

He glanced around at everyone with a fierce, angry look that was more heartrending because of the tears still trailing down his cheeks. "She was my friend, and I let her down. If it wasn't for me, Pamela Forbes would still be alive."

Oh, he definitely had the floor now. He rose, as though he

couldn't stand to stay seated one more minute. He paced, wretched and angry. "I warned her not to come here. I told her it was dangerous. But she wouldn't listen. You see, she was a woman in love."

Everyone turned to stare at Alex, who looked sullen and angry. His face reddened.

"She gave me something for safekeeping. I should have handed it over to the police, but my friendship for Alex prevented me."

He shook his head, looking almost ill with grief. "I'm sorry, Alex." And then, from his breast pocket, he pulled out a photograph. He laid it down in the middle of the table.

Naturally, everyone peered in to look at it. Dolph was the first one to speak. "But that's not Alex."

"No. It's his father."

And it was. The photograph showed Pamela coming out of a hotel, and with his arm around her, smiling down at her, was Hugo Percival Brown.

Miles pointed at Hugo with a hand that shook. "You were having an affair with Pamela. She was in love with you, and you spurned her."

There was absolute silence until Mrs. Percival Brown said, "Oh, really, Hugo. A waitress?" Her toned dripped with contempt, and I suspected it wasn't the infidelity she minded so much as the class of woman he'd committed it with.

"This is ridiculous," Hugo said, also rising. "That woman was seeing my son."

"She only went out with him to get your attention," Miles said. "She told me everything."

"Where did you get this?" He glared at Miles.

"I told you. Pamela gave it to me for safekeeping."

"That's a lie." He looked around, but everyone was staring at him. "Anyway, I was on the phone with my wife when that young woman was killed. You've got the records."

DI Chisholm said, "That's right. You were on the phone with your wife from London from ten p.m. until twenty-seven minutes past." He hadn't even checked his notes. Impressive.

Rafe nodded. "Yes, you were. But Pamela was already dead by then. That's where this didn't make sense. The timing was wrong. But you killed Pamela when you went down to get the wine with her. What happened? Did she tell you that if she couldn't have you, she was going to marry your son?"

"Dad?" Alex looked at his father as though he'd never seen him before. His face was twisted with horror.

"It's not true. Alex, Genevieve, I...this is a mistake."

Miles pushed the picture closer to the squirming man. "You killed her. I know you did."

But Hugo was a man used to keeping a cool head. He fought back. "If I killed her, then how did she get into the billiards room?"

Rafe said in a cool, expressionless tone, "You moved the body while you were talking to your wife on the phone." And that had to be the worst case of multitasking I'd ever heard.

"What? That's disgusting," his wife said.

"Of course, I didn't. This is nonsense." He rubbed the back of his hand across his mouth. "This photograph is obviously a fabrication," Hugo said. The shock was wearing off now, and I could see his brain, that same brain that had made him one of the richest men in England, was working overtime. All he had to do was refute that one piece of evidence, and there was nothing, nothing at all that connected him with the murder of Pamela.

"That boy must be insane," he said, pointing at Miles.

There was a silence hanging like noxious fumes around the table. No one moved or said another word. Miles glanced at me and then back at Hugo.

My gamble hadn't paid off. Not all of Miles's acting and not all of Hester's and Carlos's brilliance with photo manipulation had worked.

Rafe glanced over at me as though I might have something else in my back pocket. But I had nothing.

Everyone had played their part brilliantly. Miles could have received a BAFTA, even an Oscar for his performance as the grieving friend. Even I'd believe him, and I was the one who'd coached him in his scene. I could feel our chance to catch a killer slipping away. I was wracking my brains. What could I do? Was there some kind of a spell I could throw out there that might cause a killer to reveal his truth?

And then Alex stood up. Lochlan Balfour kept his eye firmly on the young man, but he wasn't trying to move. He wasn't trying to go after Jeremy. He was staring fixedly at his father.

"You slept with my girlfriend?" He was so horrified. I could see the lines of disbelief and disgust carved in his young face. "My own father? You slept with my girlfriend?"

Hugo turned to him. His face was almost purple. "No. *You* slept with *my* girlfriend." And in that moment, I saw the man snap. "You stupid fool. She was mine. She left her husband to be with me, and it all began to unravel when she realized I wasn't prepared to marry her. Oh, but she was determined." He laughed softly. "I'll give her that. It was one of the qualities I admired in her most. She had a ruthlessness and deter-mination that reminded me of myself. When I told her I wouldn't divorce my wife and marry her, she said she'd make me change my mind. I imagined the usual female attempts. Tears. Throwing herself in my path if she ever got the oppor-tunity. But oh, she surprised even me. She got to me through you. She didn't want you. Young and untried. She wanted a real man. She wanted me." He shook his head almost in disbelief.

"Chivalry. That's what this order has always been about. Sure, we get carried away and act like drunken apes, but a Gargoyle never betrays another Gargoyle. And when you took Pamela, you betrayed not only a fellow Gargoyle but your own father."

Now that he was off and ranting, there was absolute quiet in the room. I saw Ian Chisholm text something on his phone. Otherwise everyone was still.

"When she came to me for the key, that's when she told me. In the wine cellar. I'd thought she was taking me down there just to get me alone. And she was, but not for the reason I expected. Oh, she had triumph in her eyes, that girl. She said she had my son wrapped around her finger. If I didn't marry her, she was going to marry Alex. I couldn't have that."

Now it was Alex's turn to shout. "That's a lie. Why would she want an old goat like you? When she could have me?"

I spoke up now because I knew the answer to that. "It was for the title. Alex, you might be young, and you've got lots ahead of you. But the title dies with your father. If she married Hugo Percival Brown, she'd not only be unimagin-ably wealthy, but she'd be Lady Percival Brown. Pamela had lots of money, but I think she came to England for a title. She was trading up."

I looked at Hugo Percival Brown, who was panting now. His hands clasping and unclasping each other. "I think you're right, Hugo," I said, using his first name deliberately. "I think it was you she really wanted. But Pamela never cared what she had to do or who she stepped on to achieve her ends. And this time, using your own son to get to you, she took a step too far."

"I didn't mean to hurt her. It was an impulse of the moment." He looked around as though he'd been in a dream and was just coming out of it. "Alex, I—"

Alex said, "I can't hear this." He got up and left the room, and this time, no one stopped him.

Hugo turned to his wife. Before he could say anything, she snapped, "Don't say another word until our lawyer is present. You're a fool."

By this time, we could all hear the sirens. In another minute, Detective Inspector Ian Chisholm was reading Hugo Percival Brown his rights, and then the powerful man was being led away.

After the door shut behind him, Mrs. Percival Brown got to her feet. "Well, this evening's entertainment is now over. You can all get out of my house."

CHAPTER 21

"You were amazing," I said to Miles. After driving back to Oxford, we'd all gone to The Bishop's Mitre. All except Alex, that is. I suspected it would be some time before he wanted to socialize with his Gargoyle friends again. And who could blame him?

I felt vindicated, at least. I'd done the right thing by Pamela, and a killer would no doubt go to jail. Still, it was hard to imagine the Percival Brown family wouldn't be forever broken. I wondered if Alex would even continue at Oxford. But that was his business. Right now, my business was letting Miles know that his acting had blown me away.

Of course, he was lapping it up. "You didn't think the tears were a little much?"

"Honestly, my heart was breaking for you. I was the one who had coached you, and I believed you. You were absolutely amazing."

Winnie looked over at him. "What are you talking about?"

Miles glanced at me and away again. I hadn't told him the photo was a fake, but he was smart enough to get into

Oxford. He was probably smart enough to figure that part out. All he said was, "Pamela hadn't confided in me. Most of that was guesswork."

"You made all that up?"

Miles looked suitably bashful. "I did. Pamela never gave me that picture for safekeeping. But Lucy knew she was having an affair with Hugo. My job was to make him believe that Pamela had confided in me about the affair and that she'd given me that photograph."

Dolph looked stunned. "Lucy's right. That's the best acting I've ever seen. You can't go into the sugar business, mate. You've got to be an actor."

"I think you're right. Lucy, will you come with me when I tell my father?"

"I'd be delighted to."

And I thought, maybe even in darkness, something bright and wonderful would happen because of it. Miles had increased courage and confidence to stay out of his family business and go into acting.

And the way William Thresher and Violet were getting along, I wondered if something else might be beginning.

As for me? When the celebration was over, Rafe and I walked back down Harrington Street. He said, "The Percival Browns don't give one a very good example of matrimony, I must say."

"No. There aren't many couples who can stay happy, I'm sorry to say." I felt cynical and world-weary. We passed a charity box for used clothing, and I took off Pamela's scarf and pushed it into the box. At least someone would get some warmth from it.

"I was extremely happy in my marriage." He reached for my hand. "And I believe I could make you happy, Lucy."

I felt my heart pick up its pace. He turned me to him and kissed me, slowly. I pulled away slowly but kept hold of his hand. "Are you proposing?"

He chuckled softly. "I'm offering everything I have at your feet."

I was deeply honored. He'd been married only once in all the lifetimes he'd been alive. Now he wanted to marry me. If he'd been mortal, I'd be calling my girlfriends already and planning the wedding. But he wasn't. And I was.

"How can you contemplate going through that again? Loving someone, marrying them, knowing they'll live maybe another fifty or sixty years? You'd have to watch me grow old and fail and die. And you'd still be exactly as you are."

He gave me a somewhat melancholy smile. "No one knows better than I the truth of the words, ''Tis better to have loved and lost than never to have loved at all.'"

I wasn't entirely sure who had written those words, but I felt confident they hadn't been written by a vampire. "I just don't want you to end up sad and lonely."

"Lucy, I have a long, long time ahead of me. Shall I tell you the secret to living a long life?"

"Yes, please." Not that I had any interest in becoming one of the undead, but I was curious how they coped in a world that was pretty much controlled by those of us with a lifespan we could count on being less than a century.

"It's the same as how anyone should spend their life successfully. It's taking one day at a time. This very popular notion of living in the moment was discovered long ago and is still the best way I know to find happiness. I don't look at you and think of sixty years ahead. There will be challenges ahead, and we'll face them together. I look at you and see the woman I want to be with for as long as we have."

I'd had a few romantic speeches made to me in my life, but nothing could ever come close to that.

"I need time to think," I said. It was all I could manage.

He smiled wryly down at me. "I have plenty of that." We were nearly at my shop. I'd left a light burning in my flat, and the streetlight illuminated the doorway. Rafe said, "There are some very eager vampires who want to hear all about tonight."

I nodded. "And they deserve it. I'll just run up and get my knitting."

~

Thanks for reading *Garters and Gargoyles.* I hope you'll consider leaving a review, it really helps.

Read on for a sneak peek of *Diamonds and Daggers,* the Vampire Knitting Club Book 11.

~

Diamonds and Daggers, Chapter 1

"Lucy, I have decided to make you the beneficiary of my estate," Sylvia announced with drama. Of course, having been a famous stage and screen actress in the silent era, Sylvia was always big on drama.

She had come to visit me in my Oxford flat, above

Cardinal Woolsey's Knitting and Yarn shop and she was alone, which was odd. Normally she and my grandmother were inseparable. She looked at me expectantly but I wasn't sure how to react. Sylvia was a vampire so chances were that I, a mere mortal, was going to be pushing up daisies for centuries while she was still enjoying her wealth.

I sensed there was more going on here than a desire to put her affairs in order. However, I didn't want to appear rude, so I said, "Thank you."

There was a pause. She seemed to expect more. "I'm worth a great deal, you know. My jewels alone are worth a small fortune." Her lips curved in a smile. "Perhaps not so small."

I really didn't want to play games with Sylvia. She always won. So I said, "Unless there's something I don't know, you'll be wearing your jewels long after I'm gone."

"One never knows," she said vaguely. And then suddenly shifted in her chair, "Oh, all right. I need your help."

Nyx came in the window, sniffed at Sylvia's ankles and jumped onto my lap where I sat across from Sylvia on the couch. I was happy to have my familiar close while the glamorous vampire explained whatever favor she wanted.

"It's quite simple, really. A film company is remaking *The Professor's Wife*, one of my most famous films."

I knew this and she'd been furious when she found out. Now she seemed to have changed her tune. "Okay," I said cautiously.

"The company contacted my estate's lawyer, Bertram Winthrop."

Her estate's lawyer. "Is he...?"

"Undead? Oh, yes. I never do business with daywalkers. Too temporary."

"Right."

"Bertram tells me they want to pay homage to the original. They want to recreate the set of jewels used in the film."

"What jewels?"

She chuckled softly. "Cartier designed a unique set for me to wear in the movie and in the terms of my contract, I was able to keep them."

"Cartier designed jewelry especially for you."

"Of course. He was a good friend. I was paid in those jewels. The diamonds were flawless, the emeralds remarkable in color and the design is pure deco."

"Wow. That was quite the paycheck."

"I want you to wear them."

Suddenly I felt like there wasn't enough air in the room. "You want me to wear a priceless set of diamonds and emeralds? Where?"

"To London. You're to meet with the producers as my beneficiary, representing my estate."

"London?" I felt faint. There were millions of people in London and who knew how many of those were jewel thieves. "Are the jewels insured?"

"How does one insure that which is priceless?" She let that hang in the air for a moment and then said, "Don't lose them."

Order your copy today! *Diamonds and Daggers* is Book 11 in the Vampire Knitting Club series.

A Note from Nancy

Dear Reader,

Thank you for reading the Vampire Knitting Club series. I am so grateful for all the enthusiasm this series has received. I have plenty more stories about Lucy and her undead knitters planned for the future.

I hope you'll consider leaving a review and please tell your friends who like cozy mysteries.

Review on Amazon, Goodreads or BookBub.

Your support is the wool that helps me knit up these yarns. Turn the page for a sneak peek of *The Great Witches Baking Show.*

Join my newsletter for a free prequel, *Tangles and Treasons*, the exciting tale of how the gorgeous Rafe Crosyer was turned into a vampire.

I hope to see you in my private Facebook Group. It's a lot of fun. www.facebook.com/groups/NancyWarrenKnitwits

Until next time,
Happy Reading,

Nancy

THE GREAT WITCHES BAKING SHOW

© 2020 NANCY WARREN

Excerpt from Prologue

Elspeth Peach could not have conjured a more beautiful day. Broomewode Hall glowed in the spring sunshine. The golden Cotswolds stone manor house was a Georgian masterpiece, and its symmetrical windows winked at her as though it knew her secrets and promised to keep them. Green lawns stretched their arms wide, and an ornamental lake seemed to welcome the swans floating serene and elegant on its surface.

But if she shifted her gaze just an inch to the left, the sense of peace and tranquility broke into a million pieces. Trucks and trailers had invaded the grounds, large tents were already in place, and she could see electricians and carpenters and painters at work on the twelve cooking stations. As the star judge of the wildly popular TV series *The Great British Baking Contest,* Elspeth Peach liked to cast her discerning eye over the setup to make sure that everything was perfect.

When the reality show became a hit, Elspeth Peach had been rocketed to a household name. She'd have been just as happy to be left alone in relative obscurity, writing cookbooks and devising new recipes. When she'd first agreed to judge amateur bakers, she'd imagined a tiny production watched only by serious foodies, and with a limited run. Had she known the show would become an international success, she never would have agreed to become so public a figure. Because Elspeth Peach had an important secret to keep. She was an excellent baker, but she was an even better witch.

Elspeth had made a foolish mistake. Baking made her happy, and she wanted to spread some of that joy to others. But she never envisaged how popular the series would become or how closely she'd be scrutinized by The British Witches Council, the governing body of witches in the UK. The council wielded great power, and any witch who didn't follow the rules was punished.

When she'd been unknown, she'd been able to fudge the borders of rule-following a bit. She always obeyed the main tenet of a white witch—do no harm. However, she wasn't so good at the dictates about not interfering with mortals without good reason. Now, she knew she was being watched very carefully, and she'd have to be vigilant. Still, as nervous as she was about her own position, she was more worried about her brand-new co-host.

Jonathon Pine was another famous British baker. His cookbooks rivaled hers in popularity and sales, so it shouldn't have been a surprise that he'd been chosen as her co-judge. Except that Jonathon was also a witch.

She'd argued passionately against the council's decision

to have him as her co-judge, but it was no good. She was stuck with him. And that put the only cloud in the blue sky of this lovely day.

To her surprise, she saw Jonathon approaching her. She'd imagined he'd be the type to turn up a minute before cameras began rolling. He was an attractive man of about fifty with sparkling blue eyes and thick, dark hair. However, at this moment he looked sheepish, more like a sulky boy than a baking celebrity. Her innate empathy led her to get right to the issue that was obviously bothering him, and since she was at least twenty years his senior, she said in a motherly tone, "Has somebody been a naughty witch?"

He met her gaze then. "You know I have. I'm sorry, Elspeth. The council says I have to do this show." He poked at a stone with the toe of his signature cowboy boot—one of his affectations, along with the blue shirts he always wore to bring out the color of his admittedly very pretty eyes.

"But how are you going to manage it?"

"I'm hoping you'll help me."

She shook her head at him. "Five best-selling books and a consultant to how many bakeries and restaurants? What were you thinking?"

He jutted out his bottom lip. "It started as a bit of a lark, but things got out of control. I became addicted to the fame."

"But you know we're not allowed to use our magic for personal gain."

He'd dug out the stone now with the toe of his boot, and his attention dropped to the divot he'd made in the lawn. "I know, I know. It all started innocently enough. This woman I met said no man can bake a proper scone. Well, I decided to show her that wasn't true by baking her the best scone she'd ever tasted. All right, I used a spell, since I couldn't bake a scone or anything else, for that matter. But it was a matter of principle. And then one thing led to another."

"Tell me the truth, Jonathon. Can you bake at all? Without using magic, I mean."

A worm crawled lazily across the exposed dirt, and he followed its path. She found herself watching the slow, curling brown body too, hoping. Finally, he admitted, "I can't boil water."

She could see that the council had come up with the perfect punishment for him by making the man who couldn't bake a celebrity judge. He was going to be publicly humiliated. But, unfortunately, so was she.

He groaned. "If only I'd said no to that first book deal. That's when the real trouble started."

Privately, she thought it was when he magicked a scone into being. It was too easy to become addicted to praise and far too easy to slip into inappropriate uses of magic. One bad move could snowball into catastrophe. And now look where they were.

When he raised his blue eyes to meet hers, he looked quite desperate. "The council told me I had to learn how to bake and come and do this show without using any magic at all." He sighed. "Or else."

"Or else?" Her eyes squinted as though the sun were blinding her, but really she dreaded the answer.

He lowered his voice. "Banishment."

She took a sharp breath. "As bad as that?"

He nodded. "And you're not entirely innocent either, you

know. They told me you've been handing out your magic like it's warm milk and cuddles. You've got to stop, Elspeth, or it's banishment for you, too."

She swallowed. Her heart pounded. She couldn't believe the council had sent her a message via Jonathon rather than calling her in themselves. She'd never used her magic for personal gain, as Jonathon had. She simply couldn't bear to see these poor, helpless amateur bakers blunder when she could help. They were so sweet and eager. She became attached to them all. So sometimes she turned on an oven if a baker forgot or saved the biscuits from burning, the custard from curdling. She'd thought no one had noticed.

However, she had steel in her as well as warm milk, and she spoke quite sternly to her new co-host. "Then we must make absolutely certain that nothing goes wrong this season. You will practice every recipe before the show. Learn what makes a good crumpet, loaf of bread and Victoria sponge. You will study harder than you ever have in your life, Jonathon. I will help you where I can, but I won't go down with you."

He leveled her with an equally steely gaze. "All right. And you won't interfere. If some show contestant forgets to turn their oven on, you don't make it happen by magic."

Oh dear. So they *did* know all about her little intervention in Season Two.

"And if somebody's caramelized sugar starts to burn, you do not save it."

Oh dear. And that.

"Fine. I will let them flail and fail, poor dears."

"And I'll learn enough to get by. We'll manage, Elspeth."

The word banishment floated in the air between them like the soft breeze.

"We'll have to."

Order your copy today! *The Great Witches Baking Show* is Book I in the series.

ALSO BY NANCY WARREN

The best way to keep up with new releases, plus enjoy bonus content and prizes is to join Nancy's newsletter at NancyWarrenAuthor.com or join her in her private Facebook group Nancy Warren's Knitwits.

Vampire Knitting Club: Paranormal Cozy Mystery

Tangles and Treasons - a free prequel for Nancy's newsletter subscribers

The Vampire Knitting Club - Book 1

Stitches and Witches - Book 2

Crochet and Cauldrons - Book 3

Stockings and Spells - Book 4

Purls and Potions - Book 5

Fair Isle and Fortunes - Book 6

Lace and Lies - Book 7

Bobbles and Broomsticks - Book 8

Popcorn and Poltergeists - Book 9

Garters and Gargoyles - Book 10

Diamonds and Daggers - Book 11

Herringbones and Hexes - Book 12

A Spelling Mistake - Book 3

A Poisonous Review - Book 4

Toni Diamond Mysteries

Toni is a successful saleswoman for Lady Bianca Cosmetics in this series of humorous cozy mysteries.

Frosted Shadow - Book 1

Ultimate Concealer - Book 2

Midnight Shimmer - Book 3

A Diamond Choker For Christmas - A Holiday Whodunnit

Toni Diamond Mysteries Boxed Set: Books 1-4

The Almost Wives Club

An enchanted wedding dress is a matchmaker in this series of romantic comedies where five runaway brides find out who the best men really are!

The Almost Wives Club: Kate - Book 1

Secondhand Bride - Book 2

Bridesmaid for Hire - Book 3

The Wedding Flight - Book 4

If the Dress Fits - Book 5

The Almost Wives Club Boxed Set: Books 1-5

Take a Chance series

Meet the Chance family, a cobbled together family of eleven kids who are all grown up and finding their ways in life and love.

Chance Encounter - Prequel

Kiss a Girl in the Rain - Book 1

Iris in Bloom - Book 2

Blueprint for a Kiss - Book 3

Every Rose - Book 4

Love to Go - Book 5

The Sheriff's Sweet Surrender - Book 6

The Daisy Game - Book 7

Take a Chance Boxed Set: Prequel and Books 1-3

Abigail Dixon Mysteries: 1920s Cozy Historical Mystery

In 1920s Paris everything is très chic, except murder.

Death of a Flapper - Book 1

For a complete list of books, check out Nancy's website at NancyWarrenAuthor.com

ABOUT THE AUTHOR

Nancy Warren is the USA Today Bestselling author of more than 100 novels. She's originally from Vancouver, Canada, though she tends to wander and has lived in England, Italy and California at various times. While living in Oxford she dreamed up The Vampire Knitting Club. Favorite moments include being the answer to a crossword puzzle clue in Canada's National Post newspaper, being featured on the front page of the New York Times when her book Speed Dating launched Harlequin's NASCAR series, and being nominated three times for Romance Writers of America's RITA award. She has an MA in Creative Writing from Bath Spa University. She's an avid hiker, loves chocolate and most of all, loves to hear from readers!

The best way to stay in touch is to sign up for Nancy's newsletter at NancyWarrenAuthor.com or www.facebook.com/groups/NancyWarrenKnitwits

To learn more about Nancy and her books
NancyWarrenAuthor.com